"I think if I'd already met you, then we'd met on board, I would have had to walk back off the ship. Close quarters with you, Ivy Ross, is an exquisite kind of torture. Particularly with a guy who is supposed to be your boss."

She licked her lips. "What if I promise never to use that position to my advantage? You judge me on my work and my conduct—" her eyes flickered to the door "—only beyond that door, of course."

She watched him bristle at those words. He was so close she could feel his breath on her cheek. His lips brushing against her ear as he spoke. "This could be dangerous."

"This could be very dangerous." Her fingers touched the side of his face. She breathed in, inhaling his scent. Yep. She was smitten. From the smell of his aftershave, to the sensual tension in the room, she would be reliving this moment for the next five years.

"Who says I kiss on the first date?" she whispered.

"I do," he replied as his lips found hers. Warm, soft and with complete determination.

Dear Reader,

I wrote this book through one of the busiest periods of my life. My characters tend to have tragic pasts, but this time I asked my lovely editor if I could try something that started a bit lighter because my brain wasn't quite in the space for tragedy. Thankfully, she was very supportive—thank you, Carly—and I was grateful to write something that took me away to a very different time and place.

Books often transport me to another world, and I'm aware that's often what a reader needs. Travis and Ivy's story is set in the middle of the Pacific Ocean on a naval aircraft carrier. Their first meeting is a shock, as they had previously been flirting via a dating app, and coming face-to-face in a confined space leads to a rapid rise in temperature!

This was a fun story to write and just what I needed. Hope you enjoy it just as much as I did!

Love,

Scarlet Wilson

HIS BLIND DATE BRIDE

SCARLET WILSON

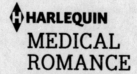

HARLEQUIN
MEDICAL
ROMANCE

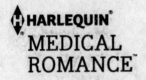

HARLEQUIN®
MEDICAL
ROMANCE™

Recycling programs
for this product may
not exist in your area.

ISBN-13: 978-1-335-40422-0

His Blind Date Bride

Copyright © 2020 by Scarlet Wilson

This edition published by arrangement with Harlequin Books S.A.

For questions and comments about the quality of this book,
please contact us at CustomerService@Harlequin.com.

Harlequin Enterprises ULC
22 Adelaide St. West, 40th Floor
Toronto, Ontario M5H 4E3, Canada
www.Harlequin.com

Printed in U.S.A.

Scarlet Wilson wrote her first story aged eight and has never stopped. She's worked in the health service for twenty years, having trained as a nurse and a health visitor. Scarlet now works in public health and lives on the West Coast of Scotland with her fiancé and their two sons. Writing medical romances and contemporary romances is a dream come true for her.

Books by Scarlet Wilson

Harlequin Medical Romance

Changing Shifts

Family for the Children's Doc

London Hospital Midwives

Cinderella and the Surgeon

The Good Luck Hospital

Healing the Single Dad's Heart
Just Friends to Just Married?

Locked Down with the Army Doc
Island Doctor to Royal Bride?
Tempted by the Hot Highland Doc

Harlequin Romance

The Cattaneos' Christmas Miracles

Cinderella's New York Christmas

The Italian Billionaire's New Year Bride

Visit the Author Profile page
at Harlequin.com for more titles.

This book is dedicated to all my fellow
key personnel who've worked throughout the
COVID-19 pandemic with me. Here's hoping
by the time this book is out we've reached
the other side.

CHAPTER ONE

Ivy Ross curled up on her sofa and sighed at the messages on her phone. It was late, she was in her pyjamas, and her current foster dog, Ruff, was curled up on her lap.

He was pretending he was sleeping. She could tell, because every now and then he turned his head slightly and gave her the side-eye when she stopped rubbing his belly. He was a scruffy sort—like most of the foster dogs she looked after—and his origins were completely unknown. He looked like some kind of small terrier cross, with his short stature and sandy-coloured fur, and he was definitely a little temperamental.

But Ivy could deal with temperamental. She'd been Flight Surgeon so often, on a variety of navy vessels with mainly male personnel, that she took it all in her stride.

Ruff nuzzled into her leg as she lifted her phone again and tried to ignore the ache of loneliness that had settled in her stomach. She'd done it all. Pursued her dream career and made it in a workforce dominated by males. It had been her goal for so long. But it seemed that in her pursuit of her goal she'd lost a little of her life along the way.

Her phone buzzed again and she looked at the response on the dating app. Being away on regular deployments, often for months at a time, meant relationships were difficult.

Most guys she'd met—mainly very nice—weren't interested in a woman who often ended up working thousands of miles away, surrounded by hundreds of other men. And that suited her more than she let on to her friends. Having her heart broken once was enough. Being told she wasn't enough once was enough. Paul was now a distant memory in her past, but the scar that he'd left had made Ivy reconsider her whole outlook on dating and relationships.

Ivy had never mixed business with pleasure, and had always refused to date a work colleague. Too complicated. Too much hassle.

The dating app worked. It kept her friends happy and sometimes amused by the tales she could tell. But it also allowed her to guard her heart from any future hurt. The world could see she was dating, and potentially 'looking' for some kind of relationship, whilst secretly it saved her from a lot of awkward questions.

She had a one bed, one bath rented apartment on the bay of the island of Coronado, just opposite the city of San Diego. It was beautiful, if a little costly, and thankfully pet friendly, set in a complex with good facilities. The drive across the San Diego-Coronado bridge always gave her a rush of feelings of luck and belonging, to stay in such a beautiful city and be part of such a great organisation.

But lately coming home to a comfortable, but empty, apartment had left Ivy feeling lonely. Living in a beautiful place like this could be hard. She constantly heard life all around her. On a daily basis she caught glimpses of couples and families going about their everyday lives, all reinforcing the fact that she was on her own.

It had led her to dog fostering—taking a troublesome character from a local shelter for a few weeks at a time to try and help familiarise them with living in a home again, and hopefully making them more adoptable.

Ruff was number six. He was proving to be a bit more difficult than the rest, probably because he was older and seemed set in his bad habits, which involved chewing anything at all. His three-week furlough with her was due to end tomorrow and Ivy couldn't pretend she wasn't a little sad. But apparently the shelter had a family lined up to meet him, so it was all for the best.

Ivy shook her head as another message popped up in one of the other dating apps. Currently she was registered on three—all under pseudonyms. The last thing she wanted was to be discovered by one of the sailors she served with.

She frowned and swiped on her screen. The latest match had proved himself tasteless on the first message. Delete.

In the last month Ivy had become a bit of a master of these apps. She was looking for someone to date—not a five-minute fling or hook-up. She said so in all three of her profiles, but that didn't stop a few guys with other things on their minds sending her messages. She deleted them all quickly.

Another message buzzed onto her screen.

Hi Ali, hope you're doing well. Which city are you in currently? R x

She smiled and shifted on her sofa as Ruff gave a low growl at the disturbance. Rob. He was one of the few potential bright sparks on the horizon. They'd exchanged first general, then a few flirty texts for the last two months. Although they were both based in San Diego, both of them had careers that made it difficult to coordinate. Twice they'd planned a date, and twice they'd had to rearrange. Rob was an international banker and frequently flew across the US and to other countries for business. Ali, her alter ego on this app, was a specialist insurance agent who could be gone for weeks at a time.

Of course it wasn't true, but she was reluctant to reveal her true name or her true job until she'd got to know someone a little better. She wanted to be honest about being away a lot, so having an alternative job where she could be out of the picture for weeks at a time was handy.

She'd been texting three separate men for a few weeks now. But Rob was definitely the one who interested her most. He seemed down to earth. Fun. Cheeky and a little flirty.

Her fingers moved to answer.

Hi Rob, I'm home right now. Have been for the last three weeks. How about you? A x

She couldn't pretend that her stomach didn't give a little flip-flop.

Just landed. How about we try and finally have that date?

Ruff gave a yelp as Ivy sat upright, sending Ruff spilling from her lap. She glanced at her watch. It was late—but not too late.

Her fingers paused above the screen. If she answered straight away, would she seem too keen?

She stood up and walked through to her bedroom and pulled open the wardrobe doors. What to wear if she said yes? Ruff nuzzled into her legs, as if trying to remind her that she should be paying attention to him. 'Sorry, boy,' she said, biting her bottom lip as she scanned the contents of her wardrobe while trying to decide if she should answer or not.

She pulled out some jeans and a black strappy top with some scattered sequins across it.

Her phone gave another buzz and she smiled. He was waiting for her answer.

Well...?

Sure. Let's meet somewhere for a drink.

She definitely couldn't pretend her stomach was feeling normal. Ivy sighed as she caught sight of her appearance. Her hair was currently tied in an unruly knot on top of her head. It was clean. Just not styled in any way, shape or form. She pulled it loose and shook it out, flicking the switch at the wall for her straightening iron.

Her phone buzzed and she almost leapt on it. Rob had named a popular wine bar set right on the bay. It was about a fifteen-minute drive from where she stayed. As she was staring at the message on the app her phone started to ring.

Her friend Liz. She pressed the screen to chat as she started to get dressed.

'Hey, girl, what you doing?' asked Liz.

'I'm getting ready for a date,' replied Ivy as she tugged on her jeans.

'You're what!' squealed Liz.

Ivy grinned. She knew the response would get this kind of reaction. 'That guy I've been messaging.'

'Which one?' cut in Liz. 'I can't keep up.'

'Rob.'

'Ah...'

Ivy was changing her bra. 'What does that mean?' She turned and faced her phone as if Liz was actually in the room.

'He's the one you actually liked, isn't he?'

'He could be,' answered Ivy as she pulled the strappy top over her head.

'Didn't he cancel on you?' came the voice.

'Yeah, he did,' said Ivy, as she pulled a face at the memory. 'But I had cancelled on him first.'

'So this time it's for real?'

'Apparently.' Ivy was standing in front of the mirror, wondering if she'd made the right choice. 'Hold on,' she said, picking up her phone and snapping a selfie before sending it to Liz. 'What do you think? What does it say?'

She stared at her reflection critically, all the while wondering if she could actually pull her hair into some kind of shape before she had to leave.

Liz paused at the other end of the phone. 'It's good,' she said finally. 'It's "Look what I can throw on and look spectacular in". But please tell me you're going to do something with your hair.'

Ivy laughed as she tugged a comb through her blonde tangles, which objected to being tamed.

'What can I ever do with this hair?' she asked.

'Let your natural curls take over,' said Liz promptly. 'It only gets in that state when you've been straightening it too much.' There was a loud sniff through the phone. 'In fact, I can tell, I can smell the burning. You've switched them on already. Put them off. Spritz your hair with some water and get your diffuser out instead. Anyway, where are you meeting this guy? Somewhere central? Somewhere safe?'

Ivy smiled—knowing that if the shoe were on the other foot she'd be saying exactly the same things. Trust Liz. 'We're going to Gino's in Old Town,' she replied.

'Hmm, nice,' said Liz. 'Central enough, with some cosy booths and good wine. Does he know the place?'

'I take it he must,' said Ivy as she dotted some foundation on her face. 'He's from San Diego, but I'm not sure where he lives.'

'You haven't told him where you live, have you?' said Liz immediately, her tone wary.

'Of course not.' Ivy laughed. 'I'm feeling kind of bad. He doesn't even know my real name, or what I do yet.'

'Nothing wrong with that,' said Liz quickly. 'Make sure you're at least ten minutes late,' she added. 'That way you'll have time to scan the bar and make sure he's not actually one of your workmates.'

Ivy shuddered as she applied some eye make-up. 'Don't even say that. Not even funny. We've got a whole bunch of new marines who think they are fantastic. *Please* don't let it be one of them. That would be a disaster.'

She shook her head as she took out her mascara. 'No, I think Rob is who he says he is.'

'Have you done an internet search on him?'

Her hand froze. Of course she had. But she hadn't found him.

The silence gave way to a shriek from Liz that sent Ruff jumping in the air in fright.

'You have, haven't you? Ooh, you didn't find anything, did you? Well, that's weird, isn't it? Because if he's really an international banker he has to have an online presence somewhere, doesn't he?' There was another minuscule pause. 'Hey, want me to come along? Just in case he's not what you think?' Caution laced her words.

'Hey, boy,' said Ivy softly, as she took a few steps and bent down to pet Ruff. 'Didn't mean you to get a scare.' She rubbed both sides of his face as he scowled at her.

A tiny part of the shine about this date was starting to wear off as worry threaded its way through her head. Maybe she should be more cautious?

'Ivy? You still there?'

She gave Ruff another pat. 'Yes, I'm here,' she said as she stood up again and caught sight of her hair. Her hand went automatically to the straightening wand and she made a few half-hearted attempts to pull it through her stubborn natural curls.

She was watching her reflection in the mirror the whole time, but her eyes caught sight of the clock on the wall behind her. 'Darn it, I'll need to run. There's a trolley in a few minutes.'

'You're getting the Old Town trolley?'

Ivy nodded as she gave up on her hair. 'Why not?'

'Tourists,' said Liz with a shudder.

'I like the tourists. Plus, I always get a discount. And Elvis is usually on this shift,' she said. The green and orange Old Town trolleys covered a twenty-five-mile loop of the city.

Elvis was one of her favourite trolley drivers. A little eccentric, he dressed as Elvis every day while working, sometimes doing a little singalong while telling the tourists about the history of the city.

She grabbed her phone and her bag. 'Okay, wish me luck. I'd better go.'

'Message me,' said Liz quickly. 'And leave immediately if you think he's a creep.'

Ivy laughed. 'Liz, I'm not fifteen, and I can take care of myself.'

Liz sighed. 'I know you can, but I feel obliged to say it. Have fun!'

Ruff followed her to the door, looking hope-

ful. She leaned down and gave him a big hug.
'Sorry, honey.' She rubbed his coat. Truth was,
she was going to miss him when she had to
hand him back tomorrow, but having a dog
on a permanent basis with a job like hers
just wasn't on. She looked into his big brown
eyes. 'Some family is just going to love you
to pieces,' she said as she blinked back a stray
tear and stood up again. Ruff realised at this
point that she wasn't actually taking him for
a walk, shot her a look of disgust and trotted
off to a corner.

Ivy took a deep breath, slid her feet into a
pair of gold flats, glanced at her watch and
bolted out the door.

What had he done? Travis King shook his head
as he strode along the street to Gino's. It was
only a ten-minute walk from his apartment,
and the Old Town was busy as usual. It didn't
matter what night of the week it was, this part
of San Diego always had a buzz in the air and
jostling crowds.

He'd been flirting on and off with this par-
ticular woman for the last few weeks on the
app. They'd almost met, and he still felt bad
about letting her down at the last minute when
he'd been called away to duty. He'd almost
been tempted to tell her what his real job was,

rather than the description he used online at the moment of 'international banker'. That was his brother's job, so it had been easy to pick up a few tips.

His apartment had had that odd, unused odour when he'd opened the door half an hour earlier, so he'd thrown open the glass doors to his wide balcony and left them open. He'd bought the apartment a few years back, thinking he was going to be more or less permanently based in San Diego. But he'd barely signed the deal when he'd been shipped off— first to Chicago, then Washington, then Hawaii. The life of a navy surgeon was never quiet.

His phone buzzed in his pocket. On my way. He smiled. Finally. He might actually get to meet the elusive Ali, the insurance agent who seemed to jet about almost as much as he did.

He tapped his fingers on his phone, a nervous habit, and quickly shoved it back in the pocket of his jeans. It wasn't that he was anxious about the date. Of course not. He'd been on enough dates in his life to write a dating guide—some good, some bad. In his teenage years there had been the girl who'd stayed at the end of his street and after two dates had camped out in his backyard—much to the amusement of his three sisters. Then there had been the girl who'd also been dating three of his other friends. At med school he'd met a girl at a local restaurant and gone to meet her just in time for the cops to show up and arrest her for shoplifting.

Finally, there had been all the 'friends' his three sisters had set him up with, each one nice, but just not for him. It seemed to be their mission to find him a girl. In all this, his brother was no help whatsoever. Mr International Banker had married his high school sweetheart years before and had the perfect wife and two kids.

The dating app made things easy. It was a perfect cover. Since his deployment four years ago to a war zone, followed by a catastrophic fire in a hotel he was staying in, his nights had been full of nightmares, reliving one experience or the other. Sometimes the nightmares faded and settled for a while, only to rear their heads again when he wasn't expecting them. He had no real knowledge of what triggered them. All he knew was that he hadn't had a serious girlfriend in the last four years. No relationships. No overnight stays. He didn't want to share his horror with anyone else.

His last real girlfriend had stayed in Hawaii and things had come to a natural end when he'd been stationed elsewhere. She wasn't the type to wait around when he'd been deployed to a war zone and it had turned out she'd been right not to wait for him. He'd been on his own ever since, and frequently placated his sisters by sometimes showing them who he was meeting, or chatting to on the dating apps.

On the surface, it looked as though he was putting himself out there, but if the nightmares flared up too much he could delete the apps and pull himself back, protecting himself for a while. His family had no idea about his nighttime horrors, and he wasn't about to share. He was a doctor. He could deal with this himself. So he couldn't quite put his finger on why he was so edgy about this date.

Was it timing? He was hoping to be based permanently in San Diego now, and his nights had been quieter lately. Maybe things were settling down once and for all. Eventually he would like to meet someone and finally settle down to a normal life—or as much of a normal life as anyone who was in the US Navy could have.

Maybe it was his age. Most of his friends in their mid-thirties like him had met someone by now and were starting to make family plans. He'd never had those thoughts before and had no idea why they were entering his brain now.

His friends had liked the fact he seemed

to go from one date to another. It seemed to brighten up their lives. But it would be nice to stop being their light relief.

He walked into Gino's, welcoming the dim lights and relaxed atmosphere. He spoke to one of the bartenders and took a seat in a booth in the middle of the bar. Jazz music filled the air, soothing but soft. By the time he finally met Ali, he wanted to actually be able to hear her talk.

She'd given him good vibes. Confident. Self-assured. Fun. Most important, she took her job seriously—just like he did. The only thing was he had no idea what she looked like. Did that even matter?

He didn't like to think of himself as a guy who would judge someone on their appearance. A few of his friends had told him the fact she didn't have a profile pic was a red flag. But he'd been quick to point out that neither did he. It was complicated. Using a pic when he wasn't using his real name could cause all sorts of issues. There were dozens of computer programs out there that could easily scan his image and search for it elsewhere. That could end up with a whole host of uncomfortable questions. Why was a navy surgeon posing online as someone else?

Plus, at some point, he felt you just had

to have trust in someone. He had to hope he wasn't about to meet someone who was thirty years older than they claimed to be, but the possibility had circulated in his head.

He sent a quick message.

I'm here. What do you want to drink?

The answer came so swiftly he couldn't help but smile.

On the Old Town trolley. Will be at least another ten minutes. Rosé wine, please, and keep it chilled!

He raised his brows at the slightly unusual choice and scanned behind the bar to make sure they had what she wanted before he ordered. Most bars in San Diego only stocked red, white and the very occasional blush. But Gino's had a variety of rosé wines so he asked for a recommendation and hoped for the best as he carried it back to the table. A woman at the next table gave him an admiring glance but he pretended not to notice. He'd dressed in a black polo shirt and jeans. Casual. And whilst admiring glances were nice, there was only one woman on his mind right now, and he was happy to wait.

* * *

'Elvis' had broken into 'Blue Suede Shoes' moments after Ivy had boarded the trolley. Within seconds most of the passengers were singing along as the trolley made its way across the Coronado bridge. Her hair was immediately ruffled in the evening breeze but Ivy didn't really care. It clearly didn't want to be tamed and it was useless to try.

She closed her eyes for a second, leaned back and smiled. She had a good feeling about tonight. That was unusual for her. Generally, she was nervous about talking on the dating app, the whole aspect of meeting someone. Probably because on a few occasions she'd felt kind of let down later. But this time felt different.

She'd chatted with Rob for a few weeks. He seemed down to earth, had a wide range of interests and a bit of cheeky flair. She liked that. There would just be those few awkward moments when, after meeting him and ensuring she felt safe, she would have to admit what her real name and job were. It paid to be cautious in this life, and she was sure she would know pretty quickly if it felt safe to be herself or not.

She grinned as a text arrived from Rob and she answered it quickly. Her timing was perfect. He was there first.

She'd just sent the text when her phone rang.

It gave her such a shock she almost dropped it—even more so when she recognised the number. 'Ivy Ross,' she answered.

'Ms Ross, there's an emergency,' came the deep voice of her commander.

She sat bolt upright. 'What kind of emergency?'

'It's Flight Surgeon Davis on the USS *Calvin Coolidge*.'

Her skin chilled. The USS *Calvin Coolidge* was one of the biggest ships in the fleet. An aircraft carrier that could carry as many as five thousand personnel.

'What's wrong?'

'There's been an accident—not him. His wife and kids have been in a serious car accident. We have to bring him home and we need a replacement.'

'What do you need me to do?'

She could almost hear her commander smile as her stomach lurched. 'We need you to be ready to deploy at zero six hundred hours.'

Her mouth went dry. It wasn't the job. She'd done it before and enjoyed it. It was the short notice. That, and the fact she'd had her fingers crossed for promotion. She was eligible, she'd been interviewed, and she'd been hoping against hope that the next call she got from her commander would be telling her she'd be Senior Medical Officer somewhere. Taking this position would likely rule her out for any immediate new role. But Ivy always did the job she was needed to do. Her stomach had a roll of regret as she said the words. 'Where is the USS *Calvin Coolidge*?'

'In the Pacific. Pack your things, Flight Surgeon Ross, you're needed.'

Her mouth was still open as the call ended. She hadn't even asked if she would be a permanent replacement or not. How long would she be deployed? Weeks or months? It wasn't that long since she'd got back from her last assignment. She loved her job, but knew rest and recuperation were essential.

Working on the aircraft carrier would mean that as Flight Surgeon she would be responsible for the welfare of thousands of colleagues, along with the senior medical officer and chief medical officer. It was a huge deal. Every minute of every day would be filled with work. She would be permanently on call—always ready to jump at the first sign of a siren. Her last assignment had been smaller, more manageable.

This one was like throwing her straight in at the deep end. She licked her dry lips. But the commander had phoned her. He'd thought of her when disaster had happened. She didn't want to believe she was the only person qualified who could fly out a moment's notice. The US Navy didn't function like that. She could almost see the list of files on his desk as he'd deliberated the job, weighing up who was most suited. He'd chosen *her*. This time her heart missed a few beats. That was good. No, that was great.

She'd spent years wanting to finally be on the radar of the commander. She admired him and wanted to impress him. He clearly thought she was up to the task. But would he consider her for a bigger task? There was so much to think about. One thing was for sure, if she said she didn't want to take this emergency job, she would automatically tumble down the ranking for any promotion.

Her stomach flipped over as she remembered Ruff. She'd need to make arrangements for a colleague to take him back to the shelter tomorrow—and it wouldn't be open before six a.m.

A photo of a glass of wine appeared on her phone. Oh, no.

Rob. She grimaced. The wine looked perfect. Chilled, with some condensation on the glass, in the midst of a dimly lit bar—the perfect place for a first meeting. How on earth could she tell him?

Her fingers started typing before she even thought.

So, so sorry, but family emergency and I need to bail. I promise, at some point, we will actually meet.

She stood up then walked to the front of the trolley, signalling to Elvis that she needed to get off. He shook his head as they were nowhere near an official stop. The trolleys weren't supposed to stop anywhere else.

'Sorry,' she pleaded. 'It's an emergency.'

After a few moments he gave a shrug and slowed down, giving her the chance to alight. 'Don't know what you're missing,' he said with a twang in his voice as he pointed towards the heart of San Diego.

She pulled up another app to grab a ride back to her apartment, and thankfully a car was only a few minutes away.

As she jumped inside, she realised that Rob hadn't replied and a wave of regret washed over. She felt terrible. She'd been looking forward to this and now, with one call, she had to walk away. But that was her job, her duty. Part of her wished she'd been a little more truthful, then she could have actually revealed why she had been called away. But it was too late now. As the car sped back across the Coronado Bridge she turned her phone over in her hands, wondering if she'd just blown it for good.

Travis had just sat down and taken his first sip of beer, letting the cool liquid slide down his throat. He was ready for this. Ready to meet this fun-sounding woman who lived in the same city as he did, and see where it went. Maybe they could have a few fun dates? His eyes kept heading to the door—even though she'd told him she was ten minutes away.

A small woman in a red coat walked in. His pulse rate quickened. But the woman let out a squeal and ran over to another table, embracing someone in a bear hug. Travis sighed and pretended he wasn't thankful. He wasn't sure she was his type. Two women around the right age wandered in, chatting and laughing conspiratorially. One brunette, one redhead, both dressed in jeans and light shirts. Maybe Ali had brought a friend. That made sense. He could understand that. But a few seconds later two men walked in behind them and joined the ladies at the bar. They were clearly two couples.

His phone buzzed. An email. He flicked it open and sighed. Peters, a friend and colleague who'd spent the last few weeks trying to convince Travis that he wanted to look to the future—encouraging him to think about leaving the navy and setting up in private practice in San Diego. Peters had a very successful practice already but one of his partners had left recently. He was anxious to fill the spot, and he'd set his sights on Travis.

In a way it was flattering, but Travis didn't even want to think about things like that. Right now, he was focused on staying in the Navy Medical Service. He liked it. No, he loved it. He slid the email away. The limited conversations he'd had with Peters had always been after a few spells of bad nightmares. Private practice would probably be in his future at some point but things were settled right now. He didn't want to make the transition before he thought he had to.

He bent his head, trying to take his eyes off the door. It hadn't been ten minutes yet. Then his phone buzzed again. He picked it up instantly, seeing the message on his screen. His first instinct was to groan and then have a quick look around. Maybe she was in the bar, watching him, and she hadn't liked what she'd seen?

He glanced down at his clothes again and at his reflection in the gantry behind the bar. His job meant that he was physically fit. Most women considered him vaguely attractive, a few had even called him outright handsome. And, no, it wasn't just his mother and sisters. Had Ali taken one look and walked away?

The thought didn't sit comfortably with him. He looked around the bar. Sure enough, as far as he could see, he was the only person right now sitting with a glass of rosé on the table.

Travis looked around again and then laughed and shook his head. Had he missed out on some kind of girl code? Was he getting too old these days to not understand the signs?

It could be something else entirely. It just seemed well…odd that as soon as he'd sent the photo of the wine glass she'd blown him off.

Maybe she was just old-fashioned nervous. There. That was a better thought. But it still left him sitting alone in a San Diego bar.

He had asked her at short notice. But she'd been quick enough to accept. Maybe Ali did have a genuine family emergency. Maybe she would message later or even tomorrow to makes excuses and rearrange. And if she did, would he agree?

He debated in his head as more people streamed into the bar. Soft jazz music was playing around him. A few couples, some groups of friends. An older, single man who sat at the bar, sipped his beer and read the paper.

The woman at the next table gave him a coy smile. 'What's wrong? Date called off? Silly girl. I can keep you company, if you like.' She flashed her teeth at him and he drew in a deep breath.

He didn't want a companion who might want to hang around overnight. He wanted something more meaningful than that. It's why he'd spent the last few weeks getting to know Ali. It's why the first thing he'd done when he'd landed had been to text her and ask her out.

He wanted the chance to finally meet face to face. Get to know if the buzz that seemed to flicker via message between them was actually there when they met in person.

He looked at the glass of wine and empty seat opposite him, trying to think of any reason in the world why he shouldn't just look like some guy who'd been stood up. Instead, he flashed her a smile and stood up. 'Let's just say you win some, you lose some and some aren't worth waiting for.' He picked up his bottle of beer and drained it, before heading to the door and walking out into the warm evening air.

CHAPTER TWO

By the time she reached the USS *Calvin Coolidge* Ivy was exhausted. Because the aircraft carrier was already deployed she'd had to travel via a number of different methods to get there. It was not as if she hadn't flown in a dozen naval planes before. Helicopters were more familiar. But since the *Coolidge* was in the middle of the Pacific Ocean, the distance was too far to travel in one journey.

Instead, she'd found herself going from San Diego to Hawaii and then by military jet before finally landing on the *Coolidge*. It didn't matter how many times she'd seen the fighters land on aircraft carriers before, as a passenger she still had a moment of terror when it seemed like the jet might just shoot off the end of the runway.

'Here you go, Flight Surgeon.' The cheeky pilot who'd flown her in grinned. 'Welcome to our brand-new aircraft carrier.'

'Thank you, Captain Yang.' She smiled as she waited for the steps to be put in place for her to disembark.

The sun was high in the sky above them. The Pacific Ocean unblemished and stretching for miles around them. But as soon as she stepped from the jet the wind almost knocked her from her feet. One of the crewmen grinned and grabbed hold of her elbow.

'Head down, ma'am, and move in that direction.'

The door to the carrier seemed a million miles away at the other end of the flight deck. She grabbed her bag and walked in long strides, praying she'd get out of the fierce wind soon.

It was ironic really. Most of the men and women on this aircraft carrier spent weeks below deck—there were currently eighteen decks under her feet—and would probably love to get some fresh air. But right now Ivy couldn't wait to get inside.

As soon as she got through the door she dropped her bag at her feet to give herself a few seconds to catch her breath. By the time she looked up, an older guy with grey hair was looking at her. Tony Briggs. He gave her a wide smile.

'Tony!' She leaned forward and gave him a hug. 'I had no idea you were CMO on the *Coolidge*.'

He shrugged. 'It's great to see you, Ivy. When I heard you were the replacement I couldn't have been happier.' He gave her a sideways glance. 'I thought you were moving on to bigger and better things?'

She stepped back and nodded. 'It was a bit of a surprise call but...' She looked around at the never-ending views of grey walls and said with a laugh, 'How could anyone not want to do this?' Then she sighed. 'As for the bigger and better things, I guess I'll just need to wait a bit longer.'

Tony nodded. As Chief Medical Officer on the aircraft carrier, he would be her closest colleague. It was a relief that it was someone she already knew—someone she trusted and had worked alongside in the past. He'd been one of the first doctors she'd met when she'd joined the US Navy. Steady as a rock, encouraging without overstepping the line. He'd let her learn from her mistakes on more than one occasion, but had always been ready to assist and chat. He respected her just as much as she respected him.

She gave a nervous shiver as she looked

around. 'Have to be honest, didn't think I'd end up here.'

Tony gave a nod. He knew exactly what she meant without putting it into words. 'You're more than qualified. This job won't be any different than any other—just a few more people,' he added with a smile. 'Crew roll is five thousand, five hundred and thirty-two.'

She gulped and put a bright smile on her face. 'Okay.'

Tony threw back his head and laughed. 'Don't give me the "Ivy smile".'

She shook her head in confusion. 'What's the "Ivy smile"? I've never heard you say that before.'

He raised his eyebrows. 'That one where you smile at someone when it's completely clear that your brain is racing away in the background with a hundred other questions.'

She laughed and gave his upper arm a light slap. 'You know me far too well.'

He gestured his hand towards the slim corridor in front of them. 'Come on, let me show you to your quarters.'

'My closet?' she quipped back. The quarters on any navy vessel were always tiny, but she'd grown used to them.

She moved down the corridor in front of Tony, occasionally having to flatten herself against a wall to let others past, going down almost vertical stairs as they descended into the heart of the vessel.

The USS *Calvin Coolidge* was virtually new. Completed and launched the year before, it was the most modern aircraft carrier in the fleet.

Tony gave her a rundown as they moved to her quarters. 'I'll show you around the medical department and our state-of-the-art facilities once you're settled. The SMO obviously wants to meet you—you know, give you the talk about pressure and teamwork. Have you met Isaiah Bridges before?'

She shook her head. The senior medical officer would be her boss on board the carrier. He had a sterling but stern reputation. She was a tiny bit nervous about meeting him. Particularly because she wanted to be in his shoes one day.

Her phone buzzed in her pocket and she started. 'Oh, satellite's working, then?'

Tony nodded. 'Surprisingly well, unless you're in the absolute depths on the ship. You should have no problems with access.'

He pointed to a grey door to her left. 'You're in here.'

As an officer on board and with her position as Flight Surgeon, Ivy had her own quarters. To say it was compact was being kind.

But since some of the crew shared with sixty other people in three rows of bunks, having a tiny bit of space to herself was a luxury.

She dumped her bag and took off her coat. The heat inside the ship was already getting to her. It only took a few seconds to retie her rumpled hair and straighten her uniform. She would change later—if she was meeting the SMO, she wanted to impress him.

Tony gave her a nod of approval and took her back down the corridor. On naval ships the med bays and theatres were always near the centre of the ship in order to ensure the most stability. On a ship the size of an aircraft carrier there were, of course, also battle dressing stations at strategic points across the vessel to be used in case of emergency. But the med bay really was in the heart of the ship.

Tony beamed with pride as he showed her around the facilities. It was clear he was proud of how modern everything was. Ivy's stomach gave a pang of pride. She believed in the service they provided for their crew. Just because they were stuck in the middle of an ocean, it didn't mean that the crew should go without care. X-rays, blood tests, even emergency surgeries could be performed on the aircraft carrier. There was an active emergency room, a physical therapy clinic, operating room, an intensive care unit, up to sixty ward beds if required, a lab, pharmacy, X-ray room, a fully equipped dental surgery and a whole range of medical, dental and nursing staff to assist.

A tiny tremor went through her at the knowledge that if some kind of mass disaster occurred, this ship could literally be turned into a floating emergency centre. Some of the crew were also trained as medical corpsmen and could assist if required.

Ivy took a steadying breath. Things were calm today. There were a few patients in the hospital ward, others in the waiting area looking for some kind of medical advice. Although surgery was her speciality, while on board she would be expected to also deliver everyday preventative medicine to the crew. She liked that. She'd discovered early in her career that she didn't want to focus too narrowly on one speciality.

General surgery was as narrow as she'd got. But as a member of navy medical personnel she'd also had the pleasure of studying aviation and aerospace medicine and been involved in some areas of research. The variety made it one of the best jobs on the planet, in her view, and she was thankful every day.

Her mind drifted. *One day, all this could be yours.* She knew it was completely and utterly fanciful, but it had always been her dream to get as far up the ranks as she could. She wanted to be the person in charge of all this. All the medical personnel. To take responsibility for the full medical contingent on this vessel.

I can be good enough.

The words echoed in her head. Remnants of the mantra she'd kept repeating to herself ever since Paul had left. She'd hated him for breaking her heart. But now she was kind of glad it had happened. It had given her even more drive to be the best at everything she did. She was always striving to be the best doctor, the best surgeon, and focus on her career. Whilst she never wanted to lose her practical skills, she also wanted the respect and ability to use her organisational skills too.

Being SMO on an aircraft carrier was the ultimate job goal. She pressed her lips together for a second. She'd really hoped that would have been her next post. This one was like being put in a holding pattern, and she'd need to let her head accept that, and move on.

She watched as one of the nurses sat next to the bed of one of the patients, holding his hand and talking quietly to him. Relationships between crew members were always discouraged, but no one seemed to be paying too much attention. She could see the worry in the woman's eyes and the tremble in the hands of the male patient.

'What happened?' she said in a low voice to Tony.

He glanced up in the direction she was looking. 'Yeah. There was an accident yesterday. We're lucky our petty officer is still here. He put himself between a major piece of machinery and one of the seamen.'

Ivy drew in a deep breath. There was potential danger every single day whilst they were at sea. Accidents happened. But they were always investigated. As if he were reading Ivy's mind, Tony shot her a smile. 'Guess what your first job will be?'

She nodded. 'No problem. I'll see to it.' When a crew member was injured, a medic always took part in the investigation. Her heart gave a little pang as she continued to watch the pair. There was a real connection there. That special 'something'.

Her thoughts drifted back to two days before. She wished she'd had a chance to meet Rob. Even if it had only been for half an hour before she'd got the call. She would have liked a chance to put a face to the image she'd had in her head. To see if the easy manner translated into real life. To see if there was a little spark of attraction between them. Would a connection like the one she could currently see in front of her eyes ever be part of her life?

Would she be able to do that if—when—she was promoted next? Would there be space and time in her life for a relationship, or would the SMO role just encompass every part of her life?

Or would a spark just mean the chance of a broken heart again, and that feeling of not being good enough?

'Ivy, everything okay?'

Tony was looking at her with a frown creasing his forehead.

'Sure it is,' she said brightly. 'Let's carry on with the tour.'

An hour later she'd met a number of the crew in the hospital and med bay. Tony had gone back to seeing patients as she knocked on the door of the senior medical officer. 'Enter,' came the commanding voice.

Isaiah Bridges's dark skin gleamed a little as she entered the room. He was leaning over the desk as if he was studying something. It was only a few seconds before she realised his desk was spotlessly clean.

'Sir…' she said a little hesitantly.

He looked up and gave her a nod, pausing

for a second before holding out his hand to her. 'Flight Surgeon Ross, it's a pleasure to meet you. I've heard good things.'

Relief flooded through her. 'Thank you, sir, it's an honour to be here. Thank you for requesting me. I was so sorry to hear about Flight Surgeon Davis's family.'

Her commanding officer nodded. 'I've had word. His daughter has some serious injuries and has had emergency surgery. She's in ITU now, but is stable. His wife had a spinal injury and will be required to be immobilised for a few weeks to allow healing of her vertebrae.'

'Oh, no,' breathed Ivy. The accident must have been really serious.

Isaiah Bridges nodded. 'It's going to be a long haul for him. He'll be needed at home for the next few months. We were lucky you were able to replace him so quickly. I understand his wife should make a full recovery, but his daughter might require some further surgeries in a few weeks' time. All his efforts need to be focused at home.'

'Absolutely,' said Ivy quickly. 'I'm happy to be here.'

He gave a slightly uncomfortable roll of his shoulders, as if he had a crick in his neck, then reached for a glass of water. There was silence for a few moments as she waited for him to talk again. Finally, he took a file from a drawer and handed it to her. 'There are a few checklists in here that Flight Surgeon Davis left. A few notes on crew he was concerned about, and the list of other duties still to be covered.'

'No problem,' said Ivy as she took the folder. 'I'm happy to get started.'

He paused and looked at her again. 'I also hear there could be good things ahead for you.'

The words made her skin prickle in delight, and she couldn't help but smile. 'I hope so. You know what they say, good things came to those who wait. But for now I'm happy to be your flight surgeon.'

He gave a nod in acknowledgement.

'Dinner for my squadron is at seven. I'll see you then.'

It was a dismissal, and she was a little relieved. She walked back to her cabin and finally took a shower after all her travelling. Her body didn't know what time zone she was supposed to be in, and to be honest she could easily have curled up in her probably uncomfortable bunk. She towelled her hair semi-dry and left the rest to dry naturally. It was humid inside the aircraft carrier so any thoughts of straight hair would be a dim and distant dream.

She picked up her phone. The signal was good so she scrolled through her social media feeds. With a shake of her head she deleted two out of three dating apps. They were currently midway between Hawaii and the Galapagos Islands, two thousand miles from the nearest land. Dating would be a long way off.

Her fingers hesitated at the last app. This was the one where she'd met Rob. She hadn't even had a chance to message him again since she'd failed to show two nights ago. Ivy bit her bottom lip. If the shoe had been on the other foot she would have been furious. There was a good chance this guy wouldn't talk to her again. Her fingers hesitated above the phone. Was there even any point apologising when she might not be home again for a few months?

She could almost hear her elderly aunt's voice in her head. *Good manners cost nothing.* Of course she should apologise. It was the least she could do.

But what to say without revealing too much about herself?

She took a deep breath and started typing.

Travis was busy. Admin work was never his favourite part of the job but it still had to be done. He'd gone for a run at lunchtime, ignoring the blistering heat in San Diego, plastering himself in sunscreen, and pounded the surrounding pavements to try and work off some of his frustration at being stuck behind a desk.

He'd just stepped out of the shower when his phone buzzed. He ignored it—it was bound to be one of his sisters—as he poured himself a coffee. It was one of the few things in life he was fussy about. He should have gone to the coffee shop a few blocks from the base, but running and coffee didn't really mix. Next time he'd remember his portable cup.

His phone buzzed again and a flash of purple appeared on his screen. Travis frowned, remembering that messages that came through the dating app were purple. But he wasn't talking to anyone on the app—not after Saturday night's disaster.

He swiped the screen. Ali.

His first thought was pure exasperation and to delete it without reading. But that was the beauty of the modern phone—he could already see the first line of the message.

Hi Rob, huge apologies about Saturday night. I can't blame you if you're mad. I know I would be. But, honestly, I got called away at the last minute for an emergency that means I'm out of town for the next few months. But…

He stared in confusion at the dots. What else did she mean to say? As for the message, an apology was the least he deserved. His stomach clenched. His imagination could create a whole range of other possibilities. But maybe this was just the truth.

Recognition dawned as he saw some little dots on the screen. She was replying. Of course. She'd been checking he'd read the first message before she continued.

The truth is I was looking forward to meeting you. I'm bummed that we didn't actually get to see each other in person. You know how it is when you have a picture of someone in your head and you want to see if the imagined picture matches real life?

He set down the phone as he pulled his uniform back on and frowned. He hadn't been expecting that. Their messages had usually been fun and flirty, but this time she sounded more sincere. Almost like…she was at the same point in life that he was.

He sat back down and stared at the screen, not quite sure how to answer.

There were so many curt replies he could

give. Five minutes ago that was exactly how he would have answered. But now he was curious.

And here was me thinking you caught sight of me, the only guy in the bar with a glass of rosé wine, and bailed…

She wasn't the only one who could use dots. Her response was immediate.

What? OMG no. Absolutely no way. I would never do anything like that.

He smiled.

Really? You've never done that, ever…?

There was a slight pause.

Well, not any time lately…

So you're gone for the next few months?

The reply came quickly.

Unfortunately, yes. Duty calls. Let's just say I'm in a place where no land is in sight.

Now, that caught his interest. But before he had a chance to respond, she replied again.

How do you feel about a drink when I get back? I would like to try and meet. I was ready, and on the trolley on my way to meet you. My favourite driver, Elvis, was serenading us all with 'Blue Suede Shoes'.

There was something achingly familiar about the tale. While Travis sometimes used the regular trolleys in San Diego, he rarely used the Old Town, and knew instinctively that was the kind she was talking about. A few of his fellow crew had joked about the singing Old Town trolley driver called Elvis. The guy did actually exist.

Why don't you seal the deal by sending me a photo? Prove to me you're actually a real person and not a figment of my imagination.

He raised his eyebrows, imagining her reaction on receiving such a message. He did wonder if this was a good idea. But he was feeling bold. And it seemed Ali was too. What was wrong with asking for a photo?

The seconds seemed to stretch. Then a short reply.

Let me think about it.

No extra dots. No sentence unfinished. The phone on his desk rang and he reached over to answer it. Flirtations would have to wait.

CHAPTER THREE

IVY'S SKIN HAD prickled with that last message—but she didn't have time to think about it much. She had a quick flick through the photos on her phone. Too many laughter lines. A dress that was a bit revealing and might send the wrong message. Her nose too big in another. Her hair all over the place in the next. She sighed, knowing that Liz would tell her every single one of these pictures was fine and she was too critical of herself.

Finally, she settled on one. Her blonde hair was sleek and shiny. She was wearing a dark top and slim cropped trousers. The picture wasn't posed. It had been taken unexpectedly and showed her sitting at an outside table at a restaurant in San Diego, wine glass in hand, and laughing. It caught all her best angles, without looking retouched. In fact, it was a relief. That was the one she would send—if she finally decided to do it.

She made her way to the mess for dinner. The officers' mess was noisy and crowded. The medical team was in the left-hand corner of the room. A few people gave her a wave as she entered. It didn't take long to see what food was on offer for the day and make her selection. She made her way over to the long table, headed by SMO Bridges. He pointed to the space next to him.

Tony was nearest her and gave a short laugh. 'Prepare for the interrogation. And watch him, he's crafty with his questions.'

Ivy gave a good-natured smile and moved to sit next to Isaiah Bridges. She had half expected this. He wanted to make her feel welcome and part of the team. She was lucky. Not all commanders were like that.

The questions came thick and fast. Her training. Her interests. In turn she learned that Isaiah Bridges was married with a son and a daughter, and his wife worked as a producer for a TV news show. His son played basketball and his daughter planned to go to art school. He'd served for nearly thirty years and for the last fifteen he'd been SMO on an aircraft carrier. During his career he'd served on every aircraft carrier that had been in active service. How she wanted that life, and that career.

As he talked he loosened the button at his

collar, giving it a little tug. The weather in the Pacific was warm, but combined with the heat of being below deck and in a crowded space she was feeling warm herself.

As it was her first night on board, she'd worn her jacket with her uniform, wondering if the officers here would be a little more informal due to the temperature around them. Everyone at her table was wearing their jackets, but she could see others from different parts of the ship in their shirtsleeves.

Isaiah's barrage of questions slowed down, and she noticed he'd only eaten a little of their delicious dinner. She passed him the jug of water on their table. 'Everything okay?'

He gave her a smile as he shook his head. 'Ah, just a little indigestion. I think I need some air. If you'll excuse me, I'm going to head along to my quarters.' He shrugged his left shoulder as if it was uncomfortable.

Ivy already knew that the corridors were likely to be even hotter than the mess. It was easier said than done to get some air on an aircraft carrier. Most of the crew would spend their time here below decks with faint hope of feeling the brisk winds above.

She stood as he excused himself and shot Tony a look, moving swiftly from her seat as Isaiah Bridges exited the mess hall.

'Something wrong?' Tony asked her.

She gave a slow nod of her head. 'Just being cautious. Can you come with me for a minute?'

Tony nodded and grabbed the jacket that he'd put on the back of his chair. She waited until they were out in the corridor. 'I'm worried about Isaiah Bridges. I think he might be feeling unwell, but didn't want to give too much away.'

Tony's professional face fell into place straight away. 'Did he say where he's going?'

'His quarters. But I wonder if he might head to the med bay. He's not stupid.'

They started down the corridor. 'What do you suspect?' asked Tony, his steps so brisk she had to lengthen her stride to keep up.

As they turned the corner Ivy realised there was no chance to answer.

Ahead of them, Isaiah Bridges was leaning with one hand against the bulkhead in front of them, his other hand across his chest. Ivy stepped in front of him, immediately noticing the beads of sweat on his dark forehead.

'Isaiah,' said Tony, all formality lost, 'tell me how you're feeling.' He nodded to a crewman at the end of the corridor. 'Get me a chair from the med bay.'

Isaiah frowned, as if he couldn't quite process the question. 'Damn,' he muttered under his breath.

Ivy put her hand on his pulse. 'Chest pain? Indigestion? Why don't you let us take you along to the med bay and run a few tests?' She glanced around. 'Just Tony and myself. We'll look after you.'

She knew by instinct that Isaiah Bridges would hate this. She thought back frantically to this afternoon, the uncomfortable roll of the shoulders, just as he'd done at dinner this evening.

She kept talking in a reassuring manner to Isaiah as they assisted him into the hurriedly procured chair and took him along to the med bay, getting him up onto one of the trolleys.

It only took a few seconds to loosen his shirt and attach the electrodes they would need for a twelve-lead ECG. It was clear that both she and Tony were thinking the same thing. Silent MI.

Sweat continued to pour from Isaiah's forehead. They were in one of the single treatment rooms but Ivy signalled quietly to one of the senior nursing staff to assist. The nurse, Jane, gave a brief blink of recognition, then moved swiftly to take some blood.

This was what Ivy loved about her job. No matter where she was in the navy. No matter what base, what ship, the staff around her moved seamlessly, working as a team, with instructions barely needing to be given. They all knew their jobs that well. It was a privilege to be part of a team like this.

She glanced at the oxygen stats. 'Any previous asthma, or COPD?' she checked with Isaiah. When he shook his head she slipped the mask over his head and turned the oxygen flow on.

The twelve-lead printed out. 'What does it say?' said Isaiah hoarsely.

The results were clear to Ivy and she handed the printout to Tony. 'ST elevation. It looks like an inferior MI. We won't wait for the blood work. We'll just treat you to save time.'

It was essential in the case of a myocardial infarction that it was treated as soon as possible to break up the blood clot that was blocking the blood flow and allowing part of the heart muscle to die.

Within a few seconds Jane returned with an aspirin in a medicine cup—the first-line treatment for any MI.

'Can you get me some thrombolytic?' Ivy asked, naming one of the popular clot-dissolving drugs commonly used for an MI.

Isaiah was shaking his head. 'But I haven't

had any chest pain,' he said, deep furrows in his brow.

'What about that referred shoulder pain?' quipped Tony. He let out a laugh. 'Don't let it be said that you do things the traditional way.'

'I'm just glad we've caught it. We can get you treated here. Then send you to a hospital with cardiac facilities for further treatment.'

Ivy gave a slightly nervous swallow. MIs could be difficult. Lots of people required balloon angioplasty or coronary artery by-pass grafting. Whilst the facilities on the ship were state of the art, they weren't as good as a specialised cardiac unit. Isaiah could well require a different kind of treatment in the next twenty-four hours. Their goal was to treat, stabilise and move him on.

'Don't worry, we'll take good care of you.'

Jane came back to the door and gave Tony a nod, handing the thrombolytic over to Ivy. It was set up in a small pump to be delivered over the space of an hour. She connected the tubing to the IV cannula that Jane had inserted while taking bloods and started the infusion.

There was a whole host of charting to be done, but Ivy pulled up a chair next to Isaiah. Right now he wasn't her boss. Right now he was a patient. And like any patient who'd just had an MI, she knew he would be anxious.

She gave him a smile. 'Okay, so let's establish that we both know our fellow doctors and nurses make the worst possible patients. What can I do to help you right now? You know we need to monitor your obs for the next hour whilst we deliver the drug.'

Isaiah rested back against the pillows and let out the biggest sigh in the world. She got it. She really did. He still really couldn't believe this had happened to him. Ivy understood that right now Tony would be reporting to the commanding officer that the aircraft carrier's SMO was undergoing treatment and would have to be airlifted from the carrier. She could only imagine how that news was going to go down.

'Would you like me to contact your wife?'

Isaiah fixed his dark eyes on her. 'Not really. You've not met my wife. She won't take this well.'

Ivy tilted her head to one side. 'Because she's predicted it for years?'

He waved one hand in the air. 'Forget it. I stand corrected. You'll get on just fine with my wife.'

Ivy gave a knowing nod. 'Okay, so we're most likely to send you back to the hospital facilities in Hawaii. Where is your wife based? Will she need transport?'

He shook his head. 'She's still on the island.

Normally, we're in Maryland. But she's got some extended leave and was visiting family with the kids.'

He put his hand up to his chest. Ivy stood up quickly. 'Are you okay?' She glanced at his heart rate and BP on the nearby monitor. Both were holding steady.

He squeezed his eyes closed for a second. When he opened them again they looked a little watery. 'I'm fine. No pain. Just wondering what this will do to my career.'

Ivy was a little taken aback at the statement. But she knew instantly what it meant. She guessed Isaiah Bridges was in his mid-fifties. Many people completely recovered after an MI. But the likelihood was that he'd find himself landlocked and desk-bound for a considerable period of time after returning to work.

Ivy's action was instinctive. She reached over and squeezed his hand. 'The most important thing is that you get treated, and you get back to full health.'

He gave a hollow laugh. 'You know that I love being out here, don't you? I love the sea. It's why I joined the navy. I even did my medical training with the service. It's in my blood, you see.'

Ivy had heard this often throughout her career. Many of her colleagues came from families where naval service was a tradition—a way of life. She was different. None of her family had served. Ivy had always known she wanted to do medicine but had never tied it in with the idea of service. When a high school friend had enlisted early and had told her stories of the next few years, it had intrigued her, particularly when he'd told her what opportunities were available via the navy.

Isaiah narrowed his gaze and studied her for a second. It was unnerving. She glanced to make sure the pump was still administering the drug slowly and steadily. 'You never mentioned any family,' he said, with an edge to his voice that made it sound like a question.

She shifted in her chair. 'My family is good. My mum and dad stay in Colorado. My sister is a teacher in Columbia. My brother is currently in Australia. We're widespread.'

Isaiah shook his head and looked at her hand. 'You're not married?'

She gave a nervous kind of laugh. 'Not yet—but never say never.'

A frown creased his forehead. 'You've met someone?'

She opened her mouth to answer but wasn't quite sure what to say. She'd never been asked such invasive questions by her commander before.

As if he sensed how uncomfortable she was, Isaiah lifted one hand. 'What I'm trying to say—and sounding like an old fool—is I can take this...' He put his hand on his chest. 'I can take what's happened today, because I know at home I have my wife and kids waiting for me.' His voice trembled a little. 'If I never get back out to sea, I know I have my life back home. I've always had something to go home to.'

He paused for a second and gazed off into the corner. 'My wife and I—Adele—we literally bumped into each other in the street. I often wonder what would have happened if we'd never met that way. What I would have become without her, and my family.' He gave his head a gentle shake. 'I was ambitious. Cocky, probably a little too dangerous. She grounded me. Made me the person I am today.'

He took a deep breath. 'What I'm saying is don't leave it too long. Don't let the navy suck the best years of your life. I know it could have easily happened to me. You're a talented doctor. You must be, or you wouldn't be here. You have the potential to be a great SMO. But think about what you have at home. Don't let it just be *this*.' He held his hand up again and clicked

his fingers. 'Because a moment, a second and
it can be snatched away.'

She could see the emotion in his eyes. Isaiah
Bridges was never this man. He was usually
a commander of steel; his reputation was re-
nowned. But there was something about a life-
changing event. Something that made patients
re-evaluate their lives. She'd witnessed it many
times before. But this time it felt more personal. As if he was playing into the thoughts
she'd had for the last few months.

She gave a conciliatory nod and glanced
over her shoulder to ensure no one else was
listening. 'I know what you mean.' Her mouth
curved in a soft smile. 'I've been thinking
about things for a while. But…' she paused
'…it can be kind of hard to meet someone
when you've got a job like mine. My career
comes first for me. I'm hoping my next job
will be the promotion I've been waiting for.
That will put more pressure on me. And I can't
give up on that. It's been my dream for the last
few years.'

Isaiah met her smile with his own. His tone
kind, he said, 'I believe there will be someone out there for you. Someone who will be
just perfect. Maybe you'll turn a corner and
walk into him, just like I did with Adele. Or

maybe…' this time he reached for her hand and squeezed it '…there's a chance already there, and you just need to reach out and grab it. You'll get your chance for the job, Ivy. Just make sure you take your chance for life too.' He looked at the pump next to him. 'I guess I'm doing fine.'

She looked at the monitor. 'Things seem to be going smoothly. I'll stay with you until it's finished and Tony comes back, and then…' she stood up and smoothed her skirt '… I'll phone Adele. Don't worry, I'll break the news gently.'

Her phone buzzed in her pocket and she pulled it out.

Still waiting for this photo. What are you—chicken?

She bristled as she grinned. It was as if he knew her. Knew that taunting her and challenging her would bring out her competitive edge. Her fighting spirit.

Jane appeared back at the door, along with Tony. 'We'll take over now,' she said kindly. 'You must still be tired. Go and get some rest.'

Ivy paused for a second. 'Are you sure? I'm happy to assist.' Tony walked over and put his hand on her shoulder. She knew he'd served with Isaiah Bridges for a few years. He'd just had to go and tell the commander that they would need to airlift him off the ship, and that the aircraft carrier would need a new SMO. That couldn't have been easy. He probably wanted to spend some time alone with his colleague.

She gave an understanding nod. She turned to face Isaiah. 'SMO Bridges, it's been an honour. I'll go and call your wife.'

He gave her a wave of acknowledgement. 'Flight Surgeon Ross, remember what I told you.'

She disappeared down the corridor towards her quarters. 'Well, that was some first day,' she muttered to herself. Things were starting to play around in her brain. She was here. She was ready. There was at least half a chance she'd be considered to step into Isaiah Bridges's role. It made sense. Why ship someone else to the middle of the ocean if she was already here? Part of her hated the fact that it had even occurred to her. But of course it would.

It wasn't a crime to be ambitious. She just hoped someone back at headquarters would join the dots and make the decision to give her a chance. Her steps grew more confident as she went. By the time she'd reached her quarters, her phone was in her hand.

You show me yours. I'll show you mine.

Too much? Too daring? Maybe it was time to reach out and grab something.

Didn't think we were quite at that stage. Are you that kind of girl, because I'm thinking about being that kind of guy...

She burst out laughing at the cheeky response. It was exactly what she needed.

You know exactly what I mean. If I send you a photo, you need to send one back. Deal?

She had the photo ready to send if he agreed. A thought flickered across her mind. What if he backed out? If she sent her photo, and then he just...ghosted her? What if he thought she wasn't good enough for him?

Panic gripped her chest for a second. That thought was just...ugh. Then Isaiah Bridges's face flashed into her head—his expression when he'd talked about his wife and his kids. A warm feeling spread through her, but she didn't have time to dwell on it as her phone buzzed again.

Deal.

One word. How could one tiny word cause her heart to leap in her chest and her stomach do an Olympic-medal-winning backflip?

Hesitation was for fools. She took a breath and pressed Send.

CHAPTER FOUR

THE CALL CUT through the dead of night and made him leap from his bed, poised for action.

Old habits died hard.

Every hair on Travis's body stood on end. It took only a few seconds to realise that it was his phone that was ringing—not a siren. He looked quickly around his apartment, which was lit only by a thin strip of light streaming through a small gap in the blinds.

It was ridiculous. He knew it was. As a doctor he'd spent half his life on call, always ready to jump at a moment's notice. But the last few years had changed things.

First he'd been on deployment with a team in a war-torn area, acting to provide healthcare and medical aid. They'd come under mortar fire. In a heartbeat he'd lost three close colleagues and had twenty injured people around him. It had been three days of being constantly under fire before another team had rescued them. And it had left scars. In the dark space at night he constantly wondered if he could have prioritised differently, maybe saved more lives, or used his scarce supplies in a different way. Every debrief told him he'd done the best job possible—but debriefs didn't give reassurance in the middle of the night.

A few months later he'd been staying in a Chicago hotel, attending a training event. The noise in the middle of the night that time had been smoke alarms as fire had ripped through the five-star building. He'd fought his way through blinding, choking smoke, assisting people, showing them the way to fire escapes and stairs, going back time and time again to retrieve others who'd been injured in the confusion.

The local fire chief had praised him, but also called him a fool. His lungs had been smoke damaged and he'd suffered minor burns. Maybe if only one event had happened, things would be different. But because the two events had happened in such a short period of time they seemed to have left an indelible mark on his brain and senses.

He ignored the way his heart clamoured in his chest—furious with himself—and picked up his phone. 'Travis King.'

He listened carefully, only asking short questions. 'When? Who? Condition?'

In his head he was already walking out the door. He finished the conversation and pulled on his uniform, lifting the bag he always had packed and near the door. He opened the side pocket and threw in some personal items. A few casual shirts, joggers, charger for his phone and a book he was midway through. As he lifted his phone to push it into his back pocket, the photo he'd been looking at before he'd gone to sleep flashed up.

Ali. Dressed in casual clothes, a black top and jeans, with a slim gold chain around her neck and long gold earrings dangling from her lobes. Her blonde hair looked as if it had been caught in the wind and she was laughing at something someone had said to her. The picture had taken him by surprise. Ali wasn't just good-looking—she was stunning, in a natural kind of way. Her lips were coral in the photo and she was holding a glass of rosé wine—it must be her signature drink—and when he'd received the photo his eyes had widened at the whole effect.

Travis wasn't quite sure what he'd expected. He wasn't the kind of guy who judged people on their looks, but he couldn't pretend that if Ali had walked into a bar next to him, he wouldn't have taken a second glance.

He pushed the phone into his pocket as he grabbed his car keys. He had a long journey ahead. He could easily drop a few messages to Ali on the way. It might even be fun, distract him a little from the task ahead.

Ivy checked the board in the hospital ward. It gave a quick view of who was working, any outstanding tasks and how many patients were currently in the unit. She had a few jobs lined up for today. A number of the crew had spent too much time in the sun. Several needed to have irregularly shaped moles and blemishes removed. A couple needed biopsies and their lab was equipped to look at those samples. Removal was a simple procedure for a surgeon like herself. Back on land, this would be done by a specialist dermatologist, but in the middle of the ocean it was her task.

Tony gave her a nudge. 'I've assigned Medical Corpsman Donnelly to the marine operation today. It will be good for him. Confidence-building.'

She nodded. The marines on board were doing an exercise at sea today. There was always a member of the medical team assigned in case of difficulties. She'd done the job on many occasions herself. But Medical Corpsman Donnelly was a good choice. He was young, enthusiastic and eager to learn. He'd be stationed at one of the battle dressing stations and could call if assistance was required. But routine exercises took place every few days at sea. A bored and unmotivated crew wasn't good for anyone. Training was crucial for all.

'What about SMO Bridges?'

Tony glanced at his watch. 'He should be landing in Hawaii any time soon. I have a colleague who'll give us a call later to let us know how things have gone. And our new SMO will be with us shortly.'

Her heart plummeted straight down into her shoes.

'Already? That was quick!'

They hadn't even considered her for the position? She couldn't pretend she wasn't devastated. All her hopes dashed in a few words.

Tony laughed. 'Anyone would think this was a military organisation.' It was clear he hadn't even thought of her to fill the position and that hurt too.

'Who is it?' asked Ivy. 'Anyone I know or have worked with?' She felt prickly. They were sending someone else to do a job that she could have taken on herself.

'I have no idea. The commander hasn't told

me. Just sent me a message to say to expect a new SMO in the next hour.'

Ivy set up a trolley next to her. She put on her best Ivy smile. It was important not to let others know how put out she was. Jealousy and bitterness were hardly good teamwork components. 'Well, I'm going to be busy cutting out dodgy-looking moles.'

Tony shook his head at her terminology.

It prompted her to ask, 'Do you know how many words there are for mole in dermatology?'

He shook his head.

'Seventy-two,' she said with precision. 'I did a piece of work as a medical student for a professor of dermatology. I assessed every patient his department had seen in a month. Every new referral, the outcome, diagnoses, procedures and follow-up care.'

'And that's what you learned, that there are seventy-two words for mole?'

She raised her eyebrows. 'What I actually learned was that the locum service they'd brought in to help were much more effective and efficient than the staff of eight dermatologists he had working under him. But that report?' She lifted her hand and blew into her fingers. 'Disappeared in a puff of smoke.'

'I bet it did. Well, have fun. I'm off to do

some blood work on a case that's got me stumped. Talk later.'

Ivy had just finished excising her fifth mole of the day and covered the stitches with a dressing when one of the nurses stuck her head around the door. 'Have you heard?'

Ivy snapped off her gloves and started washing her hands. 'Heard what?'

'New SMO has landed. Word is he is *hot*.'

'Jenny!' said Ivy in mock disgust as she laughed. Jenny disappeared, clearly to spread the message among the rest of the staff.

Hot. Interesting word choice. One that she'd used herself just recently. About ten seconds after Rob had sent his picture and the absolute instant that Liz had answered her phone.

'What…?' Liz had asked dopily.

'Hot. Rob. He's just sent his photo. Wait and I'll forward it to you.'

She waited the obligatory few seconds then heard the shriek at the end of the phone. 'Girl! He's not hot—he's smokin'!'

Ivy had smiled at the photo of the broad-shouldered, tanned guy with dark hair and bright blue eyes.

'Do you think he's used a filter?' asked Liz. Ivy could imagine her tilting her phone and staring critically at the screen.

'I don't think so,' said Ivy. 'Though I did think about putting a filter on my photo.'

'You don't need a filter,' scolded Liz quickly. 'You're beautiful just as you are.' There was a pause. 'Do you think it could be an old picture? Maybe it was taken ten years ago.'

'Why do you always have to look for the worst in people?' said Ivy.

'Because there's gotta be a catch. A guy this good-looking doesn't have a girl someplace?' Liz's deep southern twang was getting more pronounced. 'Or maybe he does? Maybe he has a wife? Ten kids?'

Ivy sighed and leaned back on her bed. 'Stop it, will you? Let me have five minutes of thinking this guy might (a) actually exist, (b) be interested in me and (c) have no hidden agenda. I know it's a revelation, but I'd like to enjoy this just a few minutes more.'

'Don't say I didn't warn you,' said Liz, then she let out a deep sigh. 'But, honey, if this guy is the real deal, grab him and hide him someplace quick.'

Ivy cut the call and held the phone to her chest, closing her eyes and letting her imagination drift back to San Diego. Her dreams had been interesting that night.

The ship rocked and she was jolted back to reality as the surgical instruments she'd just used rattled on the silver tray. It wasn't often she felt the momentum of the sea. Aircraft carriers were normally so big that they were pretty stable to travel on.

She tidied away the instruments. They would be autoclaved and repackaged for use again. Curiosity was seeping through her. She desperately wanted to know who the new SMO was. It was likely someone who'd done the role for years. But would that be someone the staff would describe as *hot*?

'Whoa!' The noise came from the corridor outside.

Ivy stuck her head out as one of the nurses had both hands outstretched between the bulkheads. She smiled at Ivy. 'Just getting my sea legs. Don't know what's happening today.'

'Me either.' Ivy nodded. She glanced down the corridor but there was literally nothing to see, only grey bulkheads.

She clicked the cupboard doors and drawers closed in the treatment room. She might as well go back and check in the med bays. Make sure everything was okay there whilst they were experiencing some stormy weather. It was at times like these she sometimes wished there was a way of seeing outside.

Another swell hit and she almost slid along one wall, barely managing to stay on her feet.

As she turned the corner she pressed both her hands to either bulkhead—the corridors were slim enough to do that—just like her colleague had a few moments before.

There was noise from the bottom of the corridor and Tony appeared, laughing as he banged into the bulkhead. 'Trust you to bring the bad weather with you,' he joked to whoever was coming behind him.

There was a deep throaty laugh. Seconds later, a tall, broad man in uniform appeared at the end of the corridor, his face partially hidden by his cap.

His strides were long as he walked towards her.

She squinted, then frowned. No.

Ivy gave her herself a shake, unable to move her hands to the bulkhead because of the movement of the vessel.

She looked again.

The man's footsteps faltered as he removed his hat from his head.

He pulled back in disbelief. 'Ali?' he asked.

It couldn't be. It just couldn't be. Not on her ship. Not in the middle of the Pacific Ocean. Her nose twitched. Maybe her blood sugar was low—it was nearly lunchtime. She probably needed to eat.

'Rob?'

Tony's head flicked back and forth between them like some kind of kids' toy, a look of both bewilderment and amusement on his face. 'What is this? Pick a new name day?'

Neither of them answered. Rob's bright blue eyes were searing into hers. His eyes…in the flesh. So much brighter than they'd been in the photo.

Tony waved his hand, realising this was probably something he didn't actually want to know about. He put one hand out towards Ivy. 'Flight Surgeon Ivy Ross, this…' he moved his other hand '…is our new senior medical officer, Travis King.' Tony cleared his throat a little. 'Try and use real names, folks, and I'll leave you to get to know each other.'

His eyebrows were raised as he walked down the corridor, beating the hastiest retreat she'd ever seen.

She couldn't stop looking at Rob. No, Travis. What kind of name was that? A warm wash of embarrassment flooded through her. He was probably looking at her and trying to weigh up if she looked more like an Ali than an Ivy.

Her tongue was stuck to the roof of her mouth and words just wouldn't form. Being lost for words was new for Ivy. She could always hold her own. But she'd never had the experience of having a man she'd exchanged flirty messages with appear in front of her as her new boss.

This was like a bad romance movie. This wasn't real life. The guy she'd been flirting with had just walked into the job she'd wanted for herself. And, no, he wasn't that old. He must have only been an SMO for a few years himself. They hadn't sent in some old sea dog with years of experience; they'd sent her a guy from a pin-up calendar with only a few more years of experience than herself. Something burned down deep inside her.

One edge of his mouth quirked upwards. They were entirely alone in the long corridor—a seldom seen event, even on a ship as large as this. 'So, how's the insurance business?' he asked.

Her tense muscles relaxed a little and her tongue unstuck itself. She pushed the brief wave of jealousy out of her head. This had to be oddest situation in the world. Was this how he wanted to play things? Thank goodness. She'd half expected him to give her a dressing-down about the online untruths. That could be military style from a boss who wanted to make his mark.

She gave him a careful look. 'There might be a spanner in the works,' she said quietly.

'Really?' He took a few steps closer. And

she felt it. She actually *felt* it. A shimmer in the air between them. It was the way he was looking at her. The way his eyes connected with hers, and there was a hint of a smile on his face. A smile that lit up his whole face and made him even sexier than before. Or maybe it was his height, his presence—things that really didn't translate in a photo. The weight behind his footsteps, the bulk of muscles. Whatever it was, it was a whole lot *more* than she could ever have imagined.

'What's the spanner, then?' His voice was husky and low as he stepped closer again. 'Is it a little insurance fraud?' It was his turn to let his eyebrows rise. He was almost laughing now.

'Ouch,' she said in mock horror. 'I think there might have been some fraudulent activity in international banking, not just in insurance.'

'Touché,' he said, nodding slowly.

He was beginning to seem more like a Travis now. Rob was maybe too traditional a name for this guy. Travis might be a whole lot more interesting than she could ever have imagined.

They both jumped as a siren sounded. She recognised it immediately. 'Emergency team, battle dressing station seven.'

Ivy let out an expletive and turned to run towards the nearby med bay and grab some supplies. For the briefest of seconds she saw a wave of something pass over Travis's eyes. It was the tiniest of moments, but it was there. It was definitely there.

As she ran down the corridor he was so close he was almost at her back. He threw his bag into a corner in the med bay and stripped off his uniform jacket, grabbing the things she thrust towards him. 'Lead the way,' he said.

Battle dressing station seven was several decks beneath them and she ran the whole way, with Travis breathing down her neck. He kept talking as they ran. 'Any ideas?'

'There was an exercise today with the marines. One of our medical corpsmen is with them. He must have sounded the alarm.'

'It must be the weather,' murmured Travis. 'My jet nearly couldn't land.'

Wow. Because she couldn't see outside, she had no idea what it looked like. But if one of their jets carrying their new SMO almost hadn't landed, the whole aircraft carrier was clearly being affected, and now, with a potential incident with one of their teams, things must be bad.

A sharp blast of strong wind hit them, along with a steep temperature drop. Tony approached, running from another direction. Their corpsman was on the deck, surrounded by dark figures. As she pushed them aside, she could see a pool of blood.

As she dropped to her knees she could barely hear a thing through the noise of the weather outside. One of the panels in the ship was open, exposing the ship to the elements. Now she understood the noise and drop in temperature.

She immediately pressed down on the wound on the marine beneath her and shouted in Donnelly's ear, 'What happened?'

The next moment there was a bellow above her. 'Marine, is anyone still outside?'

She couldn't hear above the muffled noise, but the next minute Travis was over at the entrance along with one of the other marines and they were physically pulling someone up a line. Seconds later they pulled the man over the rim, falling back onto the floor and yelling to the other marines to seal the door.

Ivy realised there was a third guy leaning against a bulkhead with blood pouring down his forehead from an open wound.

The panel was sealed by four marines, fighting against the wind. As soon as the door was slammed, her ears popped, adjusting to the pressure change.

Travis took charge again. 'Tony,' he said, pointing to the marine with the open head wound. He himself started an immediate scan of the marine he'd just pulled back inside. 'Report, Corpsman,' he ordered Donnelly in a gruff manner.

Ivy lifted the edge of the marine's jacket, which she'd been pressing, and it only took a few milliseconds to assess the situation. 'I need a tourniquet,' she shouted, hoping someone was listening.

Donnelly started to talk next to her. 'Marine Felipe was injured during the line descent. The heavy winds threw him into the side of the ship and knocked him unconscious. Marine Ajat attempted to assist but was caught on a piece of panelling, and when they tried to pull him up, his arm was injured.'

Marine Ajat, the man currently underneath her. 'He's torn an artery,' she said, as another medical corpsman appeared and pulled a tourniquet from an emergency kit near her. She didn't need to give the woman instructions. She'd heard the conversation and immediately placed it appropriately around the upper arm to try and temporarily reduce the blood supply to allow the team to move him.

'What about you?' she asked Travis about the marine on the deck next to him.

That man was conscious but squirming under Travis's examining touch.

'Suspected fracture of the tibia,' he said. 'Can we strap this and get him up to the sick bay?' By now, their whole emergency team had arrived. All of them with equipment. When a medical emergency was sounded on the aircraft carrier the response was always immediate. No matter who was on duty or off, all responded.

'Corporal,' said Travis in a stern voice, 'I expect a full report about this.' His eyes swept to Donnelly and Ivy gave the smallest shake of her head. She could see the exchange of glances around the creased faces. She'd served with some of these men before and she could see one of the corporals was just about to challenge Travis. He was, literally, a stranger in their midst, and since he'd flung his formal uniform aside they had no idea who, or what, he was.

'This is our new SMO, Travis King,' she said as a board was slid under her marine to transport him. She kept pressing on his wound as he was lifted upwards. There was another exchange of glances. But this time there were a few nods of heads. Recognition that this was the man they wanted looking after their colleagues, and they understood the command structure.

The movement up the stairs and along the

slim corridors was a little awkward. Four staff were around each patient. They reached the hospital and took each marine to a different bay. 'We're going to need to go to Theatre.' Ivy nodded to one of the nurses. 'I need to scrub,' she said, adding to another nurse, 'Dev, take over here, and, Donna, get Theatre set up.'

Everyone moved like clockwork. Ivy didn't need to spend more time examining the wound. She'd seen the spurt of blood when she'd lifted the jacket and the immediate blood loss at the scene, which was everything she needed to. Already another medical corpsman was stripping the clothes from the marine and covering him with a gown, while yet another was inserting a cannula and running through a bag of IV fluids.

On the other side of the room she could see Tony attending to the head wound and Travis reading an X-ray. Things certainly moved fast in here.

She moved through to the theatre. Her staff were already opening the packs of equipment that she'd need. The nurse anaesthetist was ready in scrubs and checking some notes. She looked up. 'Marine Ajat. I have his details. He's grouped and cross-matched. Do you need blood?'

Ivy nodded. 'Please. I can only approximate

his blood loss, but at a guess around four hundred mils. He has a fluid line up. Let's start with one unit and take it from there.'

There was noise at her back as her patient was rolled into the theatre. She turned around in time to see Travis start to scrub behind her. Her mask was already tied to her face, so when she opened her mouth to speak he didn't notice. Instead, he gave her a professional nod. 'You don't mind me scrubbing in this time, do you, Flight Surgeon Ross?'

It wasn't really a question. It was a courtesy as other people were in the room. She gave a nod of her own head. 'Of course not.'

He was the boss. How could she actually object? It didn't really matter whether she was in a regular hospital setting or a military organisation. If a head surgeon wanted to scrub in, she'd be a fool to voice any kind of objection.

She needed to stay on the right side of her boss. More than that, she wanted him to be secure in her competence and know he could rely on her clinical judgements and skills. He would give a report on her at the end of this. Would he know she was in line to be an SMO like himself? She needed to make sure he could see that she was ready. She might not like the fact that Travis had walked into the job she wanted, but making sure she kept her nose clean and got a good report was every bit as important.

She held out her hands for her surgical gloves and moved over to the theatre table.

One of her nurses was poised at the marine's arm, still pressing on the wound. Ivy swallowed. The brachial artery was usually only injured like this from a stab or gunshot wound. She had no idea what was happening with the outside of the aircraft carrier, but it seemed that at some point a piece of sharp-edged panelling had lifted and this marine had suffered the misfortune of it ripping through his arm. She could almost picture him dangling from a line at the side of the ship, being buffeted by the strong winds and being thrown into the sharp edge.

Ivy didn't let herself shudder. She couldn't. She was the surgeon. She had to keep steady hands and a steady heart.

As soon as her colleague lifted the current wound pad, it was likely that the area would flood with blood and she would be unable to see the damage clearly. It was a tricky procedure. Worst-case scenario was that he would pump out blood faster than she could get it back into him...on an aircraft carrier they didn't have a never-ending supply of blood.

'Ready with suction?' she asked the nurse next to her.

Lynn nodded. Her eyes crinkled and Ivy knew that underneath her mask Lynn was smiling. 'We've got this, don't worry.'

The words were reassuring. Lynn had been in service for more than twenty years. She must have sensed Ivy's slight flurry of nerves and wanted to show support, and Ivy appreciated that. But if Lynn had sensed her nerves, did that mean that Travis had too?

Ivy wanted to impress her new boss. Not because of the previous flirting. That was a whole other area she'd have to get her head around.

But, just like with Isaiah Bridges, she wanted the SMO to have confidence in her, and her abilities. She was good enough. She just needed to show him that.

She didn't even look behind her to see where Travis was, she just gave Lynn a nod. 'Let's get started.'

Travis was drawing in deep breaths. He'd been in surgery hundreds of times, but he never forgot just how important it was to realise the significance of having a person's life in his hands. Most surgeons he'd met in his life had been arrogant. There was no getting away from that.

He'd always vowed never to be like that, and he liked to make sure that the people who worked for him weren't like that either.

He watched as Ivy Ross prepared herself and conversed with her scrub nurse. There was nothing about her actions that gave him concern, or almost nothing, right up until that last moment when she seemed to pause before proceeding.

Maybe she was centring herself. Focusing solely on the task at hand. It could be that his presence was making her nervous, but no competent surgeon should be nervous while being observed by another.

He waited, wondering if he should speak, but the moment passed and Ivy proceeded with the surgery. It was a difficult and slightly unusual task. This wasn't a surgery she would carry out every day—it would normally be carried out by a specialist vascular surgeon, but that was the thing about being a navy surgeon. Out here, she had to cover every speciality as competently as possible.

He stood silently, watching her technique. The patient was losing blood fast and tying off this artery was crucial. The number of blood-stained swabs was mounting as the scrub nurse tried to keep the blood vessel visible for Ivy to do her work.

'Got it!'

The words let him breathe a silent sigh of relief. She turned to face him, her green eyes bright. 'Well, that was a little sucker.'

He laughed—he couldn't help it—as Ivy and the scrub nurse laughed too. He stayed there, conscious of the other work he wanted to observe in the medical bay. He'd worked with Tony previously, but he'd checked the rota—he hadn't met any of the other personnel before, and he liked to know everyone on his team by name.

This was an initiation by fire, but at least he'd got to see performance of some key individuals and the teamwork in place right from the start. He'd have to look up Ivy's file later to learn a little more about his mysterious almost blind date.

He moved a little closer and watched Ivy continue with the delicate surgery. Her stitching was clear and deft, and now the crucial part of surgery was past it felt easier to move closer without making her feel uncomfortable.

The monitor gave a ping and the anaesthetist changed position. 'Blood pressure has dropped, heart rate increasing.'

Ivy lifted both hands and looked carefully into the wound. As she did, she spoke smoothly. 'Let's hang another unit of blood.

I think it's a delayed response to the blood already lost. There's no evidence of another bleeder.'

Good. She wasn't panicking. She was immensely calm. She signalled behind her for a stool on wheels, which one of the staff moved closer, and she perched on it. 'I'm going to wait before I fully close. Let's make sure we can get Marine Ajat stabilised. I'd hate to have to open him twice. Everyone agree?'

She looked around the theatre, waiting until each member had nodded, before finally meeting Travis's gaze. 'What about you, SMO? Do you have an opinion?'

He looked at her curiously. It was an interesting take. Was Ivy Ross a real team player—or did she lack confidence to make a decision herself? If it was the former—that she would listen to opinions that might be different from hers—he was impressed. If it was the latter—if she needed approval from others to make a decision—then it was just the opposite and he was worried.

'You're the surgeon, it's entirely your call, Flight Surgeon Ross,' he said in a steady voice.

There was a blink of silence. 'Great,' she replied, spinning around on her stool. 'Then we wait, everyone.'

It could have been awkward. But it wasn't.

Ivy chatted easily to the team around her. It only took him a few moments to remember that she'd only got here just a few days before him. Of course. She was asking the crew questions about where they lived, their families—getting to know them, the exact thing that he intended to do himself.

Apart from her eyes, the rest of her was covered. There was hardly any part of her in view, but what did seep out was her interest in her fellow crewmates, her professionalism. She asked the anaesthetist a few times for updates on Marine Ajat's condition. The extra unit of blood started to make a difference. First, his blood pressure and heart rate steadied, then eventually started to pick up. Ivy stood up. 'I'm going to close now, folks. Don't worry, I'll have you all out of here in time for dinner.'

Travis knew it was time for him to leave. He now needed to have a conversation with the commander about how an accident like this could have happened on the aircraft carrier. He glanced at the clock on the bulkhead opposite. He could take bets now that the commander had expected him to ask those questions before now. But Travis had his own way of doing things. He was going to check on all the other marines affected today and make sure he was happy with their care. Then he was going to take time to debrief Medical Corpsmen Donnelly to get a good overview of the situation, and to make sure his staff member was fine. This was his team. This was his job.

As he left the theatre he paused a moment to take a look at Ivy as she bent to close. He still wasn't sure. Was she a good team member or not?

He intended to find out.

CHAPTER FIVE

SHE HAD THE strangest feeling that she'd done something wrong. Ivy wasn't usually unnerved at work. She was settling in well, getting to know the staff and crew and learning the different ways people worked. Because Ivy was used to moving around, she was used to quickly ascertaining the most pertinent points about her teammates.

Usually within forty-eight hours she knew who the smart-mouthed folks were, the pedantic ones, the laissez-faire types, and the two levels of confidence—super-confident and likely to overextend themselves, and can't-make-a-decision, continually second-guessing themselves.

The one person she hadn't got a handle on, at all, was Travis. Others were constantly mentioning the SMO and how he'd popped in during night shift, or done one of the general clinics, but she'd hardly set eyes on him.

If she didn't know better, she might think he was actually avoiding her. But he couldn't be, could he?

She definitely hadn't imagined things. There had been a glint in his eye, a bit of teasing at the initial meeting. She'd half expected to hear from him—at least by text, if nothing else. But it seemed ridiculous that the guy who had taken up space in her head for the last few weeks, and taken the job she wanted, was now in a confined space with her, and there had been no contact at all for the past two days. She'd frantically texted Liz, asking a million hypothetical questions, and it was clear that Liz had eventually grown tired of her.

For goodness' sake, what's wrong with you, girl? Get some backbone. Go and chase that man down and ask him what the deal is!

That had exasperated Ivy beyond belief. She'd thrown herself back on her bed and sighed. Liz just didn't get it. Ivy had plenty of backbone. But this was the navy and this was her job. She could hardly chase down her commanding officer and ask him what the deal was.

Ivy sighed and sat back up on the bed. It was the middle of the night but she was still wide awake. There wasn't exactly much for her to do. There were some reports she could look at. The boring kind of stuff that she always left for last—environmental duties, or writing up the actual reports of the investigations that she'd done. The investigation part was interesting but the report? Not so much.

She pulled on a pair of scrubs she kept in her quarters—they sometimes doubled as pyjamas for her—and wandered down the corridor to the med bay.

The nurse on duty gave her a nod and a smile. 'Nothing to worry about, Ivy,' she whispered.

Ivy nodded. 'Can't sleep. I'm going to do some paperwork.'

'You must be desperate.'

Ivy rolled her eyes. 'I am.'

The nurse looked as if she might say something else but just gave a nod of her head as Ivy filled up her coffee mug and headed through to the back office.

She picked up the files and computer she needed and bumped the office door open with her bum, balancing on top her coffee and a cookie she'd found as she backed inside.

She turned around, licking her lips at the iced cookie. She hadn't realised she was hungry, and someone had clearly bribed one of the chefs on board.

As she turned she let out a yelp. The office wasn't exactly big and there was someone sitting in her chair. As she yelped her coffee spilled and her cookie started the ominous slide to the floor. But the figure jumped up and grabbed both.

Travis. It was Travis. And he was now wearing a soft white cotton T-shirt splattered with coffee.

The only light in the room was from a small reading lamp on the table. It cast shadows around the room. 'Travis, what are you doing here?'

He gave an indignant grin. 'No, what are you doing in here?'

'I couldn't sleep.' She shrugged, looking at his T-shirt and pulling a face. 'Sorry.'

He shrugged too. 'No problem, and since you asked, I'm hiding.'

'What?' She thudded down into the other small chair next to the desk. 'Why on earth are you hiding?'

'The person in the cabin next to me is clearly having a fight on the phone with their other half. Doesn't look like it'll be stopping any time soon. Sleep was not an option.'

Ivy wrinkled her brow. 'Wait, who is in the

cabin next to you?' It had to be another enlisted officer.

But Travis held up his hand. 'Don't even go
there.' He pointed to her cookie. 'Do you plan
on splitting that cookie?'

'Do you plan on giving me the best chair?'

He looked around the tiny office, the corner
of his lip turning upwards. 'Let me think about
it while I grab a coffee and a knife,' he said.

He came back two minutes later with his
coffee and she noticed that along with his
white T-shirt he was wearing grey running
shorts and a pair of trainers. It was a far cry
from his usual uniform. Of course, he was
a normal guy who wore normal clothes, but
working in a place like this it became totally
normal to only ever see people in a variety of
their uniforms. She kind of liked it.

He held up the knife.

'Is this a murder mystery?' she asked, cup-
ping her hands around the cookie. 'You need to
know that I actually sneaked this out of a con-
tainer in the ward. It's stolen property, so if we
get caught, you have to take the heat with me.'

He nodded solemnly as he sat down. 'Some-
how I think it might be worth it.'

His eyes connected with hers and she could
swear a tiny fairy ran along the length of her

spine. She couldn't help but smile. 'Okay, but I have rules about sharing.'

He laughed. 'As a guy with three sisters and a brother, I know I'm going to regret this question, but what kind of rules?'

She pointed at him. 'You cut, and I choose.'

He waved his knife in the air. 'You forget. I am a surgeon. I can cut precisely.'

She folded her arms across her chest. 'Oh, I don't doubt you can cut precisely. But can you cut *fairly*?' She emphasised the word.

Travis raised his eyebrows. 'Let's see,' he said as he leaned over the cookie. She liked this. It was totally unexpected, but from the second he'd seen her the atmosphere between them had been relaxed. Maybe she'd just been imagining that he'd been avoiding her?

'Done.' Travis sat back proudly, looking at the two halves of the cookie.

Ivy held up the plate and rotated it slowly, examining both halves before she chose. After a few seconds Travis groaned. 'Come on, my coffee is getting cold.'

Ivy kept him waiting, carefully deciding which half of the cookie she was going to select, before picking it up and taking her first bite.

She closed her eyes. 'Mmm, lovely. We're

going to have to try blackmail to find out where these came from.'

Travis nodded in agreement, although his cookie lasted two bites. 'What brings you here in the middle of the night?'

She glanced at the stack of folders on the desk. 'Couldn't sleep. There's no bar about, no movies. I've already reached level one hundred and forty-four on PlaySurgeon so I decided the only thing to do is work.'

He let out a laugh. 'Level one hundred and forty-four?'

She shrugged. 'Boredom is a terrible thing. I play it while listening to an audiobook.'

'What kind of book?'

'Usually a crime thriller. Something that makes me think.'

This was the kind of chat she'd imagined they would have had back in Gino's in San Diego, and her head was struggling to marry this up with sitting in a tiny office with her new boss.

She ran her fingers down the side of her mug. 'You don't know how much I wish this was a glass of rosé.'

She looked up and his blue gaze meshed with hers. For a moment neither of them said anything, then Travis gave a sigh. 'Maybe it was for the best we didn't meet that night.'

She couldn't help the wash of disappointment that swept over her. 'Why?'

'Because if we'd already met...' he pressed his lips together and tilted his head to one side '...who knows what might have happened?'

There it was. The buzz. The one that she'd hoped and expected to be there. Electricity simmering in the air between them. The what-if question...

She gave a slow nod and crossed her legs, wishing that she was wearing something sexier than scrubs. 'That might have proved...interesting.'

He nodded. 'Would you have told me your real name?'

'Would you have told me yours?'

They were both smiling at each other again and Ivy gave a little sigh. 'I guess I might have if...' she held up a hand and raised her eyebrows '... I decided that I liked you.' She was teasing him and she could tell that he liked it.

He leaned back in his chair and put his feet up on the desk. His coffee rested in his hands. 'Oh, so it's like that, is it? What were my chances? Do you think you would have liked me?'

She leaned back and also put her feet up on the desk, clashing with his as she took a sip of coffee and looked up through lowered lids. 'Jury's still out.'

'Are you always this sassy?'

'You have three sisters and you think this is sassy?'

She could almost reach out and grab the electricity that was in the air between them. She couldn't remember the last time she'd had a conversation like this. Flirting. Fun. With lots of sexual tension. This was even better than she'd imagined.

'True.' He nodded. He took his feet back down and leaned forward. 'Truth is, I would have told you my real name, and what I did, probably within the first five minutes.'

She paused and licked her lips before mimicking his movements. Her head rested on her hand and they were only a few inches apart.

'I think I might have done the same.'

He smiled at her. A slow, sexy kind of smile. 'Why the fake profile?'

'Probably for the same reason as you. We have serious jobs. I don't really want people to track and trace me unless I'm sure about them. One stalker was enough, thanks.'

'You had a stalker?' He pulled back and looked genuinely surprised.

She gave a brief nod. 'Bad enough that he

was prosecuted. I still have a restraining order in place against him.'

'Wow. That's serious stuff.'

She nodded. 'Thankfully I live next to a whole host of marines who have my safety on their radar. They helped when needed and got me through.'

'What about your family?'

She gave a wry laugh. 'Oh, it was before he moved to Australia, so my brother did the brother thing. He came down with a baseball bat in his car. Thankfully, again, one of the marines helped him understand he couldn't help if he landed himself in prison.'

'Were you scared?'

The question took her by surprise. Not many people had the front to actually ask something like that. She paused, collecting her thoughts before she answered. 'Yes, and no,' she admitted. 'He was creepy. I worried about him sneaking his way into my house, or having some hidden camera that could watch me when I slept. But on the few occasions he approached me on the street I wasn't scared at all.' She gave a thoughtful nod of her head. 'I could take him.'

Travis looked at her with interest. 'No wonder you didn't want your real identity out there on the dating site.'

'I just wish I had thought of it earlier. It could have saved me a lot of trouble.'

Her coffee was cold now, and she hadn't done a single bit of the work she'd intended to. But her concentration was well and truly shot. The only possible thing she could think about now was the perfect specimen in front of her. He was wearing some kind of sports deodorant. It was clean and fresh with a hint of musk. She, in turn, was wearing nothing. Not a spot of make-up, or any kind of perfume or scent. Thank goodness she'd brushed her teeth before coming along to the med bay.

'I like your hair down,' Travis said quietly. 'You have waves.'

Her hand cupped her slightly straggly curls. 'In the humidity—which I'm sure we'll see—I have pure frizz. If I spend a few hours on it I have corkscrew curls, or poker-straight hair. Just depends how the mood strikes me.'

His smile was kind of lazy. 'What did you have the night you were meant to be meeting me?'

The memory flooded back to her. The nerves, the expectation, the excitement. She gave a shrug. 'Actually, I more or less had this. You didn't exactly give me much time to get ready.'

Travis held up his hands. 'Hey, I was just

off a plane. I didn't want to waste any time. I thought I was about to meet some woman who'd been teasing me for the last few weeks by message. Instead, I ended up sad and lonely, sitting at a bar on my own.'

'Stop it!' The gentle slap of her hand made a connection with his warm skin, and instead of pulling away she just left it there. 'You thought you were getting some hottie, and instead you would have got me.' She gestured down at her pale blue scrubs, instantly remembering how underdressed she was. The words struck a pang somewhere in her heart. That hidden part of her that always felt not good enough. They'd come out without much thought. Thank goodness she'd framed it as a self-deprecating joke.

Travis moved forward, back to his earlier position where his face was only inches from hers. 'I would have been delighted to get you.' His finger lifted and gently stroked the side of her face in a touch as light as a butterfly's wings.

She didn't hide her instinct. Her face leaned naturally towards his hand. 'Who says you're not a hottie?' he whispered. The words were so soft and husky they caressed her skin. Her hand came up and closed over his, holding it there against her cheek.

'There's rules against this,' she whispered.

'I know,' he replied, but he didn't move. 'But right now I'm pretending we're not aboard the *Coolidge* in the middle of the Pacific Ocean. Right now I'm pretending we're in Gino's in San Diego and you've just drunk your rosé, me my beer, and we're wondering what happens next.'

The tiny hairs on her arms prickled. She closed her eyes and let her mind carry her off to that exact place. There she was, wearing her jeans and black top, and for some strange reason a pair of black, patent, impossibly high heels. She didn't even own such a pair of shoes but, hey, it was her dream.

'What are you wearing?' she said in a low voice.

He didn't hesitate. 'Black T-shirt and a pair of jeans.'

His other hand moved, drifting over the back of hers, his fingers intertwining with hers. 'I'm liking what I see,' she whispered. His hand moved again, this time threading through her hair. Her breath caught in her throat. She knew what happened next. And she'd never wanted something so badly in her life.

'Me too.' She sensed him move closer, even though her eyes were closed, and held her breath, waiting for his lips to come into contact with hers.

There was a noise outside. The sound of a trolley rumbling past just as the ship gave a slight roll. They both jerked apart, just in time to hear the trolley crashing off a wall.

Ivy's heart dipped in disappointment. There were voices outside. The scramble of a few of the staff catching the wayward trolley. 'Jeez, that probably woke half the patients. Get that stowed away safely. You know better than to leave equipment hanging about.'

Ivy recognised the scolding voice as belonging to Lynn, one of the nurses.

Her heart was racing in her chest, her breath pathetic gasps. She sat back in her chair—the *good* chair. 'Whoa.'

Travis looked momentarily lost. Just like he had when the alarm had gone off on his first day. And now, like then, it was so quick, so fleeting, that if she'd blinked, she would have missed it.

He gave the smallest shudder, then looked at her again. This time something had changed. No, *everything* had changed.

'Ivy,' he said in a tight voice, standing up and pulling at his T-shirt, as if he were straightening his uniform jacket. He gave a shake of his head. 'Apologies. I don't know what I was thinking. I'm your commanding officer. I'm sorry. That should never have happened. That can never, ever happen again.'

She wasn't quite sure what to say. Most of her words were stuck somewhere at the back of her throat. Her brain was working just fine. The words in there were firing back and forth. *Are you joking me? Why didn't you kiss me? What's wrong with me? How dare you? We were this close—this close!*

She stood up and swallowed, even though her mouth was bone dry.

It was as if some kind of shutter had come over his eyes. He was looking at her, without *looking* at her. Every part of her brain was telling her to be professional. Reminding her that he was her commanding officer.

Whilst there were rules in the navy, there was no coercion here. She had been a willing participant in what had just happened. But what made her stomach curl the most was the fact that if he hadn't moved she would still be in his arms.

He had changed his mind. That tiny little voice in her head spoke instantly. *You're not good enough.*

But she wouldn't listen to that voice. She wouldn't allow those feelings to flood her like they had in the past. Instead Ivy took a moment, put her hands on her hips and looked him straight in the eye. 'Don't start what you can't continue,' she said haughtily, before turning on her heel and marching out the door.

CHAPTER SIX

TRAVIS WAS TRULY the king of bad decisions. He shouldn't have started. And more importantly he shouldn't have stopped.

He could still sense the feel of Ivy's soft hair through his fingers and smell the fruit-scented shampoo she used in her hair.

He'd been lost. He'd been lost in the moment and lost in the person. For a few minutes they'd been in the bar they had supposed to have met in. Off this aircraft carrier, away from the rules and regulations that would frown on them getting together. Travis King had been away from trauma, away from surgery and away from the memories that stayed stuck in his head... almost.

Until that second when the loud bang had shot him back there. Back to the mortar fire and hiding while trying to tend to wounded colleagues. Travis knew exactly what was wrong with him. He knew it was PTSD from the mortar attack or the hotel fire. He suspected it was a combination of the two.

Sometimes a smell or sound made him momentarily freeze and relive one moment or another. Thing was, these events passed in a flash. Most people around him wouldn't even know that something had happened. But twice now, when he'd been with Ivy, he'd had a wave of something. And what's worse, he knew she'd noticed.

He was good at hiding things. He'd been doing it for the last four years. He didn't want to see a shrink or a counsellor. He didn't imagine that having PTSD on his medical record would allow his career to progress much further. Even though he knew that, in theory, it shouldn't, he had a more cynical view. He was a surgeon. A damn good surgeon. He was here because he deserved to be.

But…

Travis drew in a deep breath. He wasn't quite sure what had happened last night. Oh, he was exactly sure what he'd *wanted* to happen. But that noise had brought him to a clanging halt.

There was something about Ivy Ross. Her smile. Her shape. The flirting.

He'd spent a long time waiting to meet someone. She was right in front of him. But even considering being in a relationship seemed to trigger a warning in his brain. He was letting his guard down. Opening his mind to new possibilities.

And that was entirely where he was going wrong. Letting his guard down meant the chance of revealing parts of himself he didn't want to share. If things progressed with Ivy, how could he deal with his issues? The truth was that even though he used the apps, he hadn't actually thought he'd ever meet someone who would make him contemplate the future. A few dates then things were finished. That was how he'd played it for the last few years. No awkward questions. No expectations. But Ivy was peeling back parts of him that he wasn't sure he was ready to expose.

But there was more. She thankfully hadn't noticed that night, but he'd been reading her file. Ivy Ross had ambition. The navy liked her. She'd never had anything less than glowing reports and was being considered for the next SMO position that became vacant.

Tiny pieces were falling into place. She'd been on this ship, right here, when Isaiah Bridges had been taken ill. Instead of shipping him in, they could have given her the position that, from the look of her record, she'd earned. Of course, they would then have had the issue of having to find another flight surgeon for the *Coolidge*—Ivy might be good, but she couldn't do two jobs. He wasn't always sure how the top brass made their decisions. If they'd promoted Ivy, it might have been difficult for the existing team to think of her as SMO. Respect was sometimes hard to get in the navy. He could only imagine that they wanted her to take up her first SMO post right from the outset. That was how he had started his—and on a ship a little smaller than this one. They probably just wanted to let her first post be a bit easier than this one. A number of the SMOs were due to retire soon. Ivy would get her chance. But how did she feel about him stepping in here when she was, literally, waiting in the wings?

Travis groaned and leaned back in his chair. As SMO he had a cabin where he could actually reach out his arms and not touch the wall on either side of him. But it still felt claustrophobic. His phone pinged and he glanced down as his heart jumped in his chest, only to plummet instantly.

It was his family group chat. His mum and dad, brother and three sisters could talk for hours, and sometimes he preferred to sit it out and pretend there was no signal in the middle of the ocean.

He knew why he'd been so interested in his

phone. He was hoping for a second that it might be Ivy. But, of course, it wouldn't be. Not after how he'd treated her last night. He shook his head. He could hear all three voices of his sisters in his head if he actually told them what had happened. They would kick his...

Every time he closed his eyes he could see the furious flash in Ivy's eyes last night. The angry tilt of her chin as she'd looked him straight in the eye and put him clearly in his place.

It had turned him on more than ever.

There was so much that could go wrong here—the first thing being that he was her commanding officer. It didn't matter that their 'maybe' relationship had started somewhere else. It didn't matter that Ivy was obviously a strong independent woman who would clearly never be influenced by him to do anything she didn't want to do. There were rules, lines that couldn't be crossed.

And he'd wanted to cross them all. Completely. Truth was, he still did.

Travis looked down at his clenched fists. It was time to hit the gym in the ship. Anywhere he could take out some of this frustration that was building in his body.

Ivy was calm. She was playing a game of imaginary dodgeball. If Travis was likely to be in a place, she made sure she was elsewhere. She had a job to do. But that didn't mean they had to overlap. She'd had to do a few minor surgical procedures on some crew members and run a few of the clinics. Healthcare and preventative medicine on the aircraft carrier was essential.

The phone was ringing as she was writing up her last set of notes. 'Flight Surgeon Ross?'

'Yes, what can I do for you?'

'This is Chief Petty Officer Cho. We've had a distress call from a boat requiring medical assistance.'

Her skin prickled. 'Any details?'

'Come topside. We'll brief you when you get here.'

She paused for a second. 'Does SMO King know about this?'

'We couldn't get a hold of him, and there's no time to wait.'

That didn't sound quite right, but Ivy didn't have time to question it. She grabbed a medical pack and shouted to one of the corpsman to accompany her. Her heart was already fluttering in her chest. Medical assistance on another vessel would likely mean her ending up at the end of a cable—not entirely her favourite place to be. But there was no time for hesitation.

Before she had a chance to think much further, she was topside, wearing her helmet and thick jacket and heading to one of the helicopters. The officer shook his head at the corpsman. 'Only room for one, and time is of the essence. Go back and try and find SMO King.'

As soon as she climbed on board, she could hear through her com. 'What do you have?'

The pilot turned. 'Call for assistance. A woman has gone into hard labour.'

He flung out his arm at the blue-and-green ocean for miles around them. 'And what a place for it.'

Ivy screwed up her face. 'Why on earth would a heavily pregnant woman be in a place with potentially no medical assistance?'

The pilot shrugged and then pulled a face. 'Who said she was heavily pregnant?'

Ivy felt her stomach clench. 'Oh, no. How pregnant is she?'

She leaned back as the helicopter took off. 'Thirty—'

She didn't catch the other figure.

The co-pilot held up his hand and signalled ten minutes.

Ivy spoke into her microphone. 'Let the carrier know we'll be bringing back a premature baby and a new mother.'

There was no way she'd be able to handle this on the vessel they were flying to. She couldn't transfer a woman in heavy labour. But she could transfer a woman who'd delivered and a baby that would likely need medical support. She swallowed heavily and leaned back even further. At least that was what she hoped she would be bringing back to the carrier. Any other possibilities just weren't allowed space in her head.

'She's gone where?'

Jane looked Travis in the eye. 'She was called to an emergency. A woman...' Jane glanced at the notes on top of the incubator she was wheeling across the room '...apparently thirty-three weeks gestation has gone into premature labour.' Jane kept walking and glanced over her shoulder at him. 'They tried to call you first but you didn't answer. Where were you?'

Her eyes looked up and down the length of his body. He was wearing a T-shirt and shorts and dripping perspiration all over the hospital floor. Travis was cursing inwardly. All the frustration he'd just taken out on a punchbag in the gym, while listening to very loud rock music through his earphones, had instantly reappeared.

'Didn't you call me over the com?'

'It wasn't me that wanted you. It was the chief petty officer.'

'Darn it.' Travis started striding up the stairs. It only took moments to reach the coms centre.

'Patch me in to my doctor. I need to know what's happening,' he said briskly.

The petty officer on duty handed him a set of headphones and gave him a signal.

'Ivy, what's going on?'

She swore at him. She actually swore at him. Someone else cut in. It took Travis a few seconds to realise who it might be. The pilot. 'Your doc is a bit busy right now. We're just putting her down.'

Travis's heart skipped a beat just as Tony joined him in the coms room. His face was red. He'd obviously heard what was happening and had sprinted here, likely from the other side of the carrier.

He put his hand over the mic. 'I missed the call. Ivy is likely about to deliver a premature baby.'

Tony rolled his eyes. 'Thank goodness it wasn't me. Been a long time since I've done a delivery.'

Travis had a sickening feeling. 'I'm not sure how long it's been since Ivy did either, or if she's *ever* done it.'

He took a deep breath and sent up a silent

prayer. This could all go horribly wrong. He'd missed the call. He *did* have some experience of this, and he should have been the one on the helicopter. If he could swap places with her right now, he would do it in a heartbeat. He only hoped that Ivy would be able to deal with whatever was out there.

She could hear them as she dangled from the cable, buffeted by the Pacific winds. Talking about her as if they'd forgotten she would be listening. She was concentrating hard. But even though she was concentrating on her controlled descent, she hoped the pilot was concentrating even harder. She didn't want to end up in the blue water—no matter how calm and tranquil it looked right now.

A man was waving frantically beneath her, and he caught her feet and guided her down. There was a moment of relief as her feet hit the deck, then she unclipped and gave the helicopter a thumbs up so it could back away.

'I'm Ivy Ross. I'm a US Navy doctor. We heard your distress call. Tell me what's happening?' she asked the man quickly.

'M-my wife,' was all he stammered as he pointed at the cabin.

She didn't wait but ducked inside, unzipping the front of her flight suit. The heat was getting to her already. A woman lay on one of the side seats, panting heavily, her legs spread slightly apart.

Ivy crouched near her head. 'I'm Ivy. I'm a doctor,' she said steadily. 'Tell me your name and how many weeks you are.'

'I'm Kalia,' she breathed. 'I'm thirty-three weeks. This came out of nowhere.'

Ivy nodded, not saying all the comments that had already naturally swirled around in her head. 'How far apart are your contractions?'

Kalia gritted her teeth and grabbed for Ivy's hand.

'I need an update,' came a cool voice in her ear.

Ivy ignored it, focusing her full attention on Kalia. 'Every few minutes,' choked Kalia.

Ivy nodded. 'Okay, any history I need to know about? Problems during your pregnancy?'

Kalia shook her head.

'Is this your first pregnancy?'

Kalia nodded. 'It's too early. Will my baby be okay?'

'Update, Ivy.' She pressed her finger to her ear where her headset still was.

'Hold on.'

She turned back to Kalia. 'Your prenatal

care—any problems? Did all your scans go okay?'

Kalia frowned. 'Everything has been fine. Right up until now.' She gripped Ivy's hand as another contraction hit. Ivy could sense the panic of Kalia's husband behind her. She waved her hand at him. 'Come around here and sit with your wife. Take her hand,' she added, thinking she would need both of hers back. This delivery was probably imminent.

'Okay, Kalia. Do you mind if I examine you to make sure everything is okay?'

Kalia nodded. It only took a few minutes for Ivy to check her abdomen and determine the lie of the baby. She snapped on her gloves and did an internal examination, which showed Kalia was fully effaced and the head was already presenting.

She gave Kalia a nod and a smile. 'Everything looks good. We're going to have a baby join us soon. Do you know what you're having?'

She was talking to Kalia and her husband but she also knew that Travis could hear every word.

He started barking in her ear. 'Any issues? What do you need? How soon can you get back?'

She kept her cool and ignored him. He might

be her commanding officer but this situation demanded her full attention and she was here herself. There was no backup. Everything was on her.

'Okay,' she said smoothly to Kalia. 'On your next contraction, get ready to push. We'll have this baby here soon.'

Inside she was praying there would be no immediate issues when the baby came out. She didn't have all the equipment they would normally have in a hospital, and it had been years since she'd supervised a delivery—not since back in her training days.

In her headset she heard the helicopter was back on the ship. It couldn't hang in the air above this vessel indefinitely. It would come back as soon as it was needed.

So right now, in the middle of the Pacific Ocean, it was just her, Kalia and Kalia's husband, along with an imminent arrival.

Swirls of doubt circled her like the genie coming out of a lamp. Maybe she'd got too ambitious. Maybe she would never be an SMO. Maybe she wasn't even a competent flight surgeon and was about to make a mess of all this. For the first time in forever she actually felt seasick—an unknown for her.

There was a voice in her ear. 'You can do this, Ivy.' It was as if he'd heard her thoughts and had realised that right now she was having moments of doubt.

It sent a shiver down her spine. As if he'd just read her mind—had realised she was as nervous as could be because this was all down to her.

The tone of his voice was different too from his earlier yells. Calmer, reassuring. Totally in control. Just like she was.

In the end, the arrival went smoothly. Half an hour after she started pushing, Kalia delivered a baby girl. The baby was obviously small at thirty-three weeks. Ivy guessed between three and four pounds. There were a few moments of panic in her chest as she gave the little girl a sharp rub to try and encourage her to start breathing. She had no proper suction or even an airway for a baby this size. Finally, there was a little yelp and Ivy let out the breath she'd been holding.

She spoke into her com. 'Okay, baby is here. Breathing, but might need a little extra support. Can we arrange a transfer, please?'

Now she'd checked the baby, she clamped and cut the cord and laid the baby on Kalia's chest, knowing how important skin-to-skin contact was for both mother and baby.

She could hear Travis's voice in the background, shouting instructions. The momentary encouragement was gone.

'We'll need to check your baby properly on the ship. Are you okay with that, Kalia?'

'You want to take my baby?'

Ivy shook her head. 'No, of course not. We'll take you both.' She turned to Kalia's husband. 'But we'll need to leave you here.'

'Can I come alongside?'

Ivy knew he didn't want to be parted from his wife and new daughter, but she also knew their boat couldn't be left drifting in the Pacific. 'Let me check with the captain. I'm sure he'll be able to work something out.'

She put her hand on Kalia's shoulder. 'We'll need to transfer you up to the helicopter once it comes back. Then I'll come up with the baby. It's a little tricky, but I'll help you with the harness and talk you through it.'

Ivy ignored how dry her mouth was currently feeling. There had been no time on the way here to think about how much she hated the whole process of being lowered from, then lifted back onto the helicopter. It definitely wasn't her favourite part of the job. Dangling like a spider on a gossamer strand of web, which felt as if it could snap in an instant, was the kind of thing that kept her awake at night.

A few minutes later she heard Travis's voice

in her ear again and the sound of the chopper in the distance. 'We'll be above you shortly. I'm going to come down and escort our mum up, then you can come up with the baby.'

Ivy was stunned. 'You're coming?'

'Of course I'm coming. I should have been there in the first place.'

She didn't quite know what to think. Was he checking up on her? Or was he just annoyed he'd missed the call?

A few moments later there was a thud on the deck and Travis appeared at the doorway. He had a wide grin on his face and a harness in his hand, which he placed on the floor. He extended his hand to Kalia's husband. 'Congratulations, Daddy. You have a beautiful daughter. Have you thought about a name?'

Ivy was stunned. He was acting as if it were normal to give birth in the middle of the ocean. No recriminations. No questions about how exactly they'd ended up in this position. Just immediate congratulations. It was actually kind of nice.

He turned to her. 'Have you delivered the placenta?'

She nodded. 'Completely intact.'

He stepped closer to Kalia. 'Do you mind if I get a look at your gorgeous daughter?'

Kalia shook her head and held out slightly

trembling arms. 'Leila,' she said as she glanced at her husband. 'That's what we're going to call her.'

Travis unwrapped the baby from the makeshift shawl that Ivy had wrapped her in and gave her a quick check. Leila looked tiny in his large hands, but what amazed Ivy most was the way he cooed and talked to the baby. She was pretty sure he hadn't delivered a baby any time recently, but he acted as though this were an everyday occurrence. It was a whole side of him that she would never have imagined. She kind of liked it.

He handed the baby back and spent a few moments talking to the father and giving him instructions about rendezvousing with the aircraft carrier. It seemed that another larger ship would be passing the following day and could take all three passengers back to Hawaii, with their boat towed behind.

Ivy helped Kalia get herself back together, then helped her into the harness and gave her instructions for transporting up with Travis. She strapped Leila close to her chest, and waited for the harness to come back down for her.

Within a few moments she was swinging in the air, caught momentarily in a sharp gust of wind, on her way back up to the helicopter.

Her heart was in her mouth, as was part of her stomach. But she lowered her head and kept talking quietly to Leila throughout the whole process, ignoring the fact she hated every second of this. The baby was bundled up in a variety of blankets that Travis had brought with him and seemed entirely unperturbed by the whole situation.

Strong arms pulled them both back into the helicopter and ten minutes later they were back on the aircraft carrier. Ivy didn't want anyone to notice that her legs were still shaking.

A whole team was waiting for them just off the flight deck. Tony gave her shoulder a squeeze. 'Okay? Do you need something?'

Travis's head turned sharply, but before he got a chance to ask the obvious question Tony spoke again. 'Ivy hates the harness. She usually ends up either wearing her lunch or with vertigo for the next few days.'

Travis's look was accusing. 'You never said anything.'

Ivy shrugged as she strode towards the door. 'I had a job to do.' Trouble was, now she was on solid ground again, it was as if all the responses she'd delayed in her body were acting at once. Thirty seconds later she was sick over the side.

As Tony and Lynn sped away with the pa-

tients, Travis put his arm around her shoulder.
'Come on, I'll give you an injection.'

She wanted to object. But she could literally
feel the spinning inside her head. She already
knew this was likely to trigger a migraine tonight.

She lowered her head and walked down the
corridor with Travis, not talking. He sat her
down in one of the treatment rooms and she
stepped out of the flight suit, swaying as she
did so. He caught her again and sat her back
down. 'Wow, you get this bad. Why didn't you
say anything?'

She kept her eyes closed. It kind of helped
her head to stop spinning. 'You weren't around.
I had a job to do.'

She stood up quickly and headed to the
sink, putting her hands on either side of it as
her stomach heaved again. He pulled back her
hair, which had become disentangled from her
ponytail band, and waited patiently. This was
truly her at her worst. But he was still there.
By her side. Later, she'd probably wonder what
it all meant, but right now she just wanted to
lie down. The sickness sensation passed and a
glass of water was pressed into her hand.

'Let me give you something for the sickness,' he said quickly.

She opened her eyes and then shut them

again. 'I'll need something for a migraine too.' Then she let out a sigh of exasperation. 'In fact, don't. I'm on duty tonight.'

'Oh, no, you're not. The only duty you might have tonight is as a patient.'

'No way,' she said as one jab, then another, nipped the skin at the top of her arms. Boy, he didn't mess around.

'If you won't stay in a hospital bed, you'll have to agree to one of us checking on you.'

Ivy sagged back down onto the hard stool. 'As long as I drink a cup of hot tea and lie down for a few hours, I'll be fine.'

Tony appeared at the door. 'She'll also need either a large slice of chocolate cake or something similar in a few hours or she gets very cranky. Believe me, I know.'

Travis looked at Tony in surprise. 'You knew about this and didn't tell me?'

Tony shrugged. 'What's to tell? It hadn't come up. Anyway, just letting you know we've had to put Leila on some supplementary oxygen. I'm sure it'll only be for a few hours but we'll keep her under observation.' As he turned to leave he glanced over his shoulder at Travis. 'I'll watch the new patients if you take care of this one. Find her some cake for later.'

Ivy grimaced. She hated being fussed over, but she was more annoyed about showing weakness in front of her new boss. A flight surgeon who hated helicopter descents was probably not on his list of prized staff skills. She expected him to say something snide, but instead he gave a big sigh. 'I'm sorry, Ivy.'

Her eyes flew open and fixed on his. 'What?'

'They put out a staff call for me, and I never heard it. I was in the gym with a set of earphones in. I missed it,' he admitted. 'It should have been me on that flight, not you.'

She gave the briefest shake of her head, knowing to keep her movements small. 'No, it shouldn't. You're SMO. This was always a task you should have delegated to one of the other doctors.'

He kept his gaze steady. 'But if I'd known about your vertigo, I would never have sent you. And when was the last time you delivered a baby?'

She swallowed, wishing she had that tea she wanted. 'About nine years ago,' she admitted.

'So, even though it wasn't your area of expertise, and it was a procedure that makes you unwell, you went anyway?'

'It's my job,' she said steadily. 'There was no time for delay.'

His gaze hadn't moved from hers. 'You didn't even try to put out a call for me or Tony?

Are you sure we haven't delivered a whole host of babies between us?'

'I know Tony hasn't. Have you?'

Travis gave a small nod. 'One or two. On my last tour of duty I think I had seven.'

'Seven!' Now she was wishing she *had* waited and tried to put another call out for either of them. Maybe then her stomach wouldn't be swishing about as badly as her head. He shook his head.

'But that was four years ago. Not recent at all.'

She closed her eyes again. The bright lights in the room were starting to nip at her eyes.

'Let me walk you back to your cabin.'

He had moved right next to her and she jumped at his soft voice. 'I should check on Leila,' she said. But even she could hear how weary her voice sounded.

His arm slipped around her shoulder. 'I'm going to walk you back to your cabin, make you tea and find you cake.'

She gave a quiet laugh and put her hand up to her head. 'Wait, did I drop into the ocean? I feel as if I'm hallucinating.'

'You didn't fall into the ocean and I don't think you're hallucinating. Or maybe you are? Need me to do a check?'

His arm felt comfortable around her shoulders, not intrusive at all. Which was odd. She'd decided she didn't like Travis any more, and he'd annoyed her. She moved her hand up to meet his, sliding her hand into his. She didn't care what it looked like, or what he might make of it. Right now, she just needed something to hold on to. 'No, don't do that. I don't need a check.' The start of the migraine was already draining her. 'I just want to get back to my cabin,' she admitted.

'Your wish is my command,' said Travis as he started guiding her down the corridor.

Ivy knew that if anyone saw them like this there would likely be talk. But she really didn't care. All she wanted to do was lie down and drink hot tea, and maybe, in a little while, eat some cake.

Before she could think much more Travis opened the door to her cabin and guided her inside. 'I'll go and get you tea. I can't give you anything else for the migraine, though.'

She nodded. 'I know. The injections are the only things that work for me. That, and sleeping for a few hours. Honestly, I'll be as right as rain in no time.'

He smiled at her expression. 'I'll also hunt you down some cake.'

She lay down on the bed once he'd left and let out a sigh. Then threw any caution to the wind and stripped off her uniform, pulling on a pair of soft pyjamas. She honestly didn't care what she looked like right now. Apart from the migraine and vertigo, she was just so grateful to relax every muscle in her body that had been tense since she'd gone out on the mission.

Within a few moments Travis came back and pressed a cup of hot tea into her hands. She sipped it gratefully. She'd been angry with him before, but he'd actually been nice to her through all of this. 'You might not be so bad after all,' she whispered as she finally drifted off to sleep.

Travis's head was all over the place. Work was fine, apart from the overwhelming guilt he'd felt that Ivy had gone on that mission instead of him. Both mother and baby were being closely monitored. Though there were a few minor hiccups, they were nothing that an extra night in the carrier's hospital couldn't solve.

He'd managed to cram all his other duties into the space of a couple of hours. He'd made a special request to the kitchen and they'd whipped up a whole cake for their hero doctor who'd gone to deliver the baby. By the time he'd collected the chocolate frosted cake and made more tea, Ivy had been sleeping for nearly three hours. He paused outside her door. Was three hours enough?

He tapped slightly at the door and pushed it open. The lights were dimmed and Ivy was still sleeping, curled on her side on top of her bed in the pair of pyjamas that hugged her body in a way he'd tried not to notice earlier. He hesitated, wondering if he should leave her, but her nose twitched and she rubbed her eyes.

She didn't change position but her green eyes blinked open and she smiled. 'Is that chocolate cake?' she asked.

He nodded.

'And tea?'

'Don't say I can't multitask.'

She smiled and pushed herself up. 'Give me a second.' She grabbed a bottle of water and her toothbrush and disappeared for a moment, looking a bit more awake when she returned. She waved her toothbrush in the air. 'Sorry, habit of a lifetime. I have to brush my teeth as soon as I wake up.'

'No problem,' he said. He'd put the cake and tea on her desk but he was sitting in her chair, so she sat on the bed opposite him.

'Okay, who did you pay to make cake for you?'

He shook his head as he lifted a large knife. 'Oh, no, I didn't need to pay anything. Ivy

Ross is now a legend on board. The doctor who delivered a baby in the middle of the ocean? The whole carrier is talking about you. I just had to ask the kitchen and they were happy to oblige.'

Her blonde hair was rumpled and she had a pillow crease on her face. He tried not to think about just how cute that made her look. She stretched out her pinkie and leaned over and stuck it in the little extra frosting at the bottom of the cake. She put in her mouth. 'Mmm... delicious.'

He stared at her. 'I can't believe you just did that.'

She looked at him in mock horror. 'Of course I just did that. It marks the cake as mine. What, did you think I was going to share? I thought you said you had sisters?'

He laughed. 'Ah...the sibling move. A wise one. I might have done that myself on a few occasions.'

She nodded. 'Just be glad I didn't stick my finger right in the middle of it.' She gave a smiling shrug. 'You can have a piece from the other side.'

He cut them slices and put them on two plates, waiting until she'd settled back with her tea and the cake on her lap before sitting down again himself. She had a little more colour in her cheeks now.

After a few bites she gave him a wary smile. She was still annoyed. She couldn't pretend she hadn't been hurt by his actions, but he certainly seemed to be trying to make up for it.

A relationship on board a ship, particularly with a colleague, was probably a bad idea—a very bad idea. It was why, when other similar possibilities had raised their heads, she completely ruled them out. But this felt different because they'd been getting to know each other beforehand—before any of this, and before they'd known each other's real identities.

She took another bite of her cake. It was going down well. 'What do you think would have happened if we'd actually gone on that blind date?'

She could have kept things simple and stuck to chat about work. But she didn't want to. If she wanted to work easily with Travis, they had to deal with this.

There was no one else around so they wouldn't be disturbed. It was just her and him in her cabin. It was now or never.

Travis made a little choking noise as his cake obviously stuck at the back of his throat, and Ivy burst out laughing. 'Sorry, did I make that go down the wrong way?'

He laughed too and shook his head, leaning back in her chair. 'You just like to keep me on my toes, don't you?'

There it was. That teasing tone. The one that had completely drawn her in, whether it was spoken or in texts. The thing that had made Travis King something more than a potential blind date. Even if that had never been her intention.

She gave an easy shrug. 'Why not?' She held up her hands. 'It's not like there's much else to do around here.'

She was joking, and he'd know she was joking. But shipboard life was so different from being back at home where bars, cinemas, open air and long walks could easily fill her life.

Travis sat his tea on her desk and folded his arms. 'I think,' he started as he raised his eyebrows, 'if we'd gone on a blind date before meeting here, it would have been an absolute disaster.'

Really? What was it with this guy? Had none of his sisters taught him the art of talking to a woman? The words were like being hit with a tidal wave of icy water.

'Okay, then,' she said shortly, feeling like a fool, because in her head their blind date would never have been a disaster.

He held up one hand. 'No, wait, you didn't

let me finish. Let me tell you why it would have been a disaster.'

She swung her legs off the bed. 'I don't need microscopic data on why we're a never-happened,' she said, pushing her 'not good enough' feelings away again.

He reached over and put his hand on her knee. His voice was low and throaty. 'Our date would have been a disaster, Ivy Ross, because one meeting would have had me hooked. Who knows what might have happened? It keeps me awake enough at night just thinking about it.'

And just like that the tidal wave of icy water dashed back out the door, to be overtaken by a stampede of warm air washing over her skin.

Her gaze met his. She was sure that the noise in the room had just amplified one hundred per cent. Was that the beat of his heart she could hear?

She shuffled a little further forward. Part of her brain was screaming at her. She'd got this close before only to have the rug pulled from under her feet. She didn't want to get burned twice.

'For a guy with sisters, you certainly know how to mess with a girl's mind,' she said, tilting her head to one side.

He had the grace to look embarrassed, but it didn't stop him moving a few inches closer.

'I think if I'd already met you, and then we'd met on board, I would have had to walk back off the ship. I never actually expected to meet someone on the dating app. I was looking for some light-hearted company. Nothing serious. Just some chat. But being in close quarters with you, Ivy Ross, is an exquisite kind of torture. Particularly for a guy who is supposed to be your boss.'

Her head was swimming. His feelings about the apps were entirely the same as hers. Short-term. Not serious. No chance of a long-term relationship. And, although he hadn't said it out loud, no chance to get hurt. She licked her lips. 'What if I promise never to use that position to my advantage? You judge me on my work and my conduct.' Her eyes flickered to the door. 'Only beyond that door, of course.'

She watched him bristle at those words. He was so close she could feel his breath on her cheek, his lips brushing against her ear as he spoke. 'This could be dangerous.'

'This could be very dangerous.' Her fingers touched the side of his face. She breathed in, inhaling his scent. Yup. She was smitten. From the smell of his aftershave to the sexual tension in the room, she would be reliving this moment for the next five years.

'Who says I kiss on the first date?' she whispered.

'I do,' he replied as his lips found hers. Warm, soft and with complete determination. His hand slid to the back of her head as their kiss deepened and her arms fastened around his neck. There was a brief movement and she found herself sitting on his lap, where she knew his intentions were far from honourable.

His hand made contact with the skin under her comfortable pyjama top and she didn't mind one bit. This could easily go much further. And the truth was, for the first time in forever, she wanted it to.

But a tiny red flag of caution waved in her mind. She couldn't pretend that her past experience hadn't made her extra-cautious. She wished she could throw that part of herself away. But it was the new her. One she had to live with. She thought she knew Travis, but did she really? And if things went downhill, she was stuck on this aircraft carrier with him as her boss for the next few months. Nowhere to run, nowhere to hide.

She pushed back gently on his shoulder.

She gave him a playful smile. 'Rob?' she said, using his fake name. 'Or Travis King, I feel as if you owe me.'

He gave her a lazy kind of smile. 'Owe you

what? At this point, you can have whatever you want.'

She nodded slowly, liking those words. 'In that case, what I want is my blind date. We might need to make our own bar. But I'd like to get dressed up. I'd like you to get dressed up too. I'd like there to be low background music.' She pointed one finger at him. 'I'd like there to be snacks. I'd like a chilled glass of rosé wine.' She slid her fingers through his short hair for a moment. 'And I'd like the man sitting opposite me to spend all his time wondering what might come next.' She leaned forward and whispered in his ear, 'Just like I will.'

At her last word she swung her legs off him and stood up, giving him a few moments to collect himself.

She wondered how he would react. But Travis took it well, readjusting his clothing as he stood up and gave her a thoughtful nod. 'A date. *Our* blind date. I think I can do that.' A sexy smile nudged at his lips as his nodding increased. He gave her an appreciative look. 'I kind of like that idea.' His brow furrowed a little. 'When?'

She pulled up her phone and checked their schedules. 'Okay, Saturday night looks good.' She gave him a cheeky wink. 'Unless, of course, I get a better offer.'

He gave a kind of half groan.

She held up her finger. 'Or, of course, if my boss sends me out in a helicopter again on a daring sea mission.'

He rolled his eyes. 'Saturday is six days away.'

She kept smiling as she walked over to open her door, letting her hand brush against his. 'It is, isn't it? Just think of the anticipation.'

He didn't even try to hide his groan. 'Saturday night it is.' He leaned close to her ear. 'Can't wait.'

His eyes drifted back across the cabin and Ivy moved quickly. 'Oh, no. Thanks for looking after me, SMO King, but you don't get to take the chocolate cake with you.' She picked it up, wrapping her arms around it. 'This is definitely all mine!'

He left with a laugh and she could hear it echo as he walked down the corridor.

Saturday night was a million miles away. But she knew this was for the best. And she was right, anticipation would make it seem even more delicious.

CHAPTER SEVEN

He'd been played like a fiddle.

And he liked it.

It didn't matter what he told himself in his head—about how it was best if he stayed away from Ivy Ross. His body didn't listen. She was like a magnet to him. He had already been cursing himself when he'd learned she'd gone out on the mission without hesitating, but when Tony had told him that the helicopter descent and retrieval actually made her ill, he could have punched himself.

Ivy's pale, wobbly form, which she'd tried her best to hide when she'd come back, just made him admire her all the more. She hadn't even radioed in for assistance with the delivery, had just handled it calmly, while probably dreading the transfer back to the carrier the whole time. The girl had courage.

He'd checked up on Kalia and her daughter and made arrangements to get them back to Hawaii. It wasn't his job to lecture them on their journey, so he left that to the captain of the carrier. No one had mentioned him helping Ivy back to her cabin, but he had noticed a few sidelong glances.

Gossip spread fast on a ship. It was like its own little village. He could only hope that their date some days later would go unnoticed. He'd already managed to procure some rosé wine. There was a strict no-alcohol policy on aircraft carriers. But on stretches of more than forty-five days crew were allowed two drinks. By next week, that time would have arrived.

Work was busy, but he and Ivy seldom worked together. A few fights had broken out on board and he'd found himself tending to a set of broken knuckles and several broken noses and a few sailors had found themselves in the brig to cool off.

Over the last few nights Travis had suffered from terrible nightmares. A few years ago he'd had lots of broken nights but that had finally settled to only one or two a month. But now, for some reason, they seemed to have returned with a vengeance. It resulted in his feeling continually tired and occasionally snappy. He hated being like that at work. Two of his sisters had already asked him what was wrong as soon as they'd seen his face when they'd video-messaged him. He'd made a variety of excuses and brushed them off.

'Travis, can we chat?' Aileen was a qualified psychiatrist but also one of the staff counsellors on board the vessel. She had two files in her hand.

'Sure,' he said, gesturing towards his office.

She sat down in a chair and crossed her legs. 'What can I help you with?'

She handed over the first file. 'Petty Officer Brooks is demonstrating some signs of depression and anxiety. I've suggested some medications for him and wondered if you'd agree. He has a few other pre-existing medical conditions, which is why I'm checking.'

Travis glanced over the file and careful notes. 'Seems reasonable. There should be no contraindications between his meds. I'll arrange to dispense the prescription. Will you be able to review him?'

She nodded. 'For now, on a weekly basis. I'll let you know if I have any concerns.'

'Will he require a change of duties?' As SMO, Travis could ask for staff to be moved without explaining why to their commanding officers.

She shook her head. 'Not yet, but I'll let you know.' She handed him the second file. He blinked when he saw the name. It was his.

The SMO's medical file was only accessible to a few people on board the ship. Aileen was one of those people.

'What's this?'

Her hands were folded in her lap. She looked him straight in the eye but her posture was relaxed. She wasn't nervous about having this conversation and weirdly that made him feel slightly nervous.

'It's been seven years since we last served together.'

He gave a nod. He remembered those days well.

'A lot has happened since then.'

'Even without this?' She pointed to the file. 'I can tell.' She let her words hang in the air between them.

'What's your point, Aileen?' He was more abrupt than he'd normally be, but all his defence mechanisms were slamming down in front of him.

One of her eyebrows rose just a fraction. 'My point is…' she took a breath '… Travis King, you might not know this, but you're human. We all are. And we are all affected, in different ways, by events we're exposed to.'

'What's that supposed to mean?' He hated how snappy he was being.

She gave a gentle shake of her head. 'It

means that my door is always open, Travis, that's all.'

She stood up before he could say anything else, pausing with her hand on the door. 'Our new doctor…' she said slowly.

'Yes?'

Aileen smiled. 'I like her. I like her tenacity and her spirit. I heard her telling off one of the pilots who was trying to act like a big shot.'

'Who was it?' The words were out before he had a chance to think.

Aileen laughed. 'Oh, you don't need to know. Ivy dealt with him appropriately. All I'm saying is that she's a good fit for this crew. She's earning their respect by just being herself and gaining some admirers.'

Travis shifted uncomfortably in his chair. 'You think?'

She nodded. 'I know, people talk. Now, remember, my door is always open.'

His initial abruptness had faded. 'I know,' he said apologetically. 'Thank you.'

She gave a nod and disappeared out the door. Travis leaned back and folded his arms. He wasn't quite sure what he should worry about first. The fact that Aileen could obviously see changes in him or the fact that Ivy had more admirers than just him.

He grinned. It was a challenge. Not Ivy as

such but the date. He would have to make sure
he pulled out all the stops to make their new
blind date as good as it could possibly be.

He could do it. And he would.

The soft navy blue dress had been found rolled
in a crumpled ball at the bottom of one of her
bags. She wasn't even sure why it was there.
She had packed some civilian clothing, but
that wasn't one of the items. It must have been
there since her last trip to New York with some
friends. She shook it out. The short-sleeved,
knee-length dress had resembled a crumpled
rag, but Ivy knew it could come out looking
brand new in the laundry. At present, it was
hanging in front of her. The fake wrap-around
look meant the dress fell in soft folds creating
a V in front, with a split near the knee to give
a hint of leg.

She had a pair of small heels that would have
to do. It felt strange dressing up while being on
the ship. It would feel even more weird, walking between her cabin and Travis's looking like
this. She might throw her uniform dress jacket
over the top to try and be a little less obvious
about what she was doing.

He'd insisted they meet in his cabin instead
of hers—although she wasn't quite sure why.
This week had been like a game of cat and

mouse between them. On the very few occasions they'd been working around each other she'd tried her very best to act casual. But her body seemed to have forgotten what 'casual' was.

Every now and then their eyes would meet and one or the other of them would flash a private smile. Whenever Travis had done it, Ivy had instantly felt embarrassed, as if a siren with giant bright red arrows pointing to their heads had been wailing and flashing around them. It had sent tingles down her spine, which was entirely ridiculous.

But all this, the lead in, the anticipation, had been building on a daily basis. She'd done this. She'd wanted it to be this way. But the delicious torture had been driving her crazy.

She grabbed some long gold earrings and shook out her hair. She hadn't even attempted to straighten it. The atmosphere on the ship would mean that even though she had a gallon of product on her curls, they would edge towards frizz in a few hours. The dress hugged her curves in a way she didn't quite remember. She'd thought it was a pretty plain dress, but right now it looked anything but plain.

She glanced at the clock. The majority of the crew would be in the mess right now, drinking their two regulation beers. It was unlikely, though, that she would get down the corridors unnoticed. This was still a working naval ship, and there were always crew on duty.

Ivy finished with a slick of red lipstick and threw her jacket over the dress, stepping out into the corridor. She kept her head low as she strode along quickly. The first corridor was, luckily, empty, as was the second. The third had two men at the end of it, talking intently over something on a tablet screen.

She was beginning to think this might be easier than she'd imagined. The thought had just crossed her mind when she heard a voice behind her. 'Looking good, Doc.'

She turned and gave a nod of her head at the young petty officer second class. He had a cheeky grin on his face and she probably should have reprimanded him, but she had other things on her mind.

Her footsteps echoed down the passage, making her feel more and more self-conscious. She tugged at the dress, wondering if it was a bit too short.

Her hand paused as she lifted it to knock on Travis's door. Her stomach was doing flip-flops. Maybe she should back out? It was obvious that their feelings were intensifying in this close-knit, pressured environment. What had happened to her vow to never date a colleague?

For a few seconds she was torn. Was six days of anticipation just a smokescreen? How well did she really know Travis?

Before she had a chance to think any further the door opened and all her previous thoughts dissolved.

Travis had a welcoming smile on his face and a spark in his eye. He was dressed completely in black—black trousers and a black fitted shirt that showed off all his best assets.

Every finger, toe and hair on her body tried to cross to prevent there being a chance of any kind of emergency on this ship for the next few hours. She wanted his undivided attention.

Travis reached out a hand and pulled her inside.

Her breath caught in the back of her throat. The whole cabin had been transformed. Not that she'd seen the inside of Travis's cabin before, but she knew it was the same as every other in this corridor.

Except this one was entirely different.

She looked around. The plain grey walls were covered in something—a printed paper with a dark wooden pattern on it. She wanted to reach out and see exactly what it was. The same paper covered his bed, which had been transformed into one side of some kind of homemade booth. A dark table was directly in front, and on the table were a covered lantern and a couple of flickering candles. There were also some plates with bar snacks, two bottles of beer and a bottle of rosé wine. All three bottles were slightly smudged with condensation, showing they'd been chilled.

As she looked around she saw there were also a couple of old-style Italian posters on the wall. Although the lighting in the room was dim, seeing the posters struck a spark in her brain.

'Gino's?' she gasped. 'You made us Gino's?'

He held out both his hands. 'You wanted us to recreate our blind date.' He gave a little bow. 'Your wish is my command.'

Of course they could never really capture the true essence of the wooden booths in Gino's and the dim atmosphere. But as she looked around in amazement Travis flicked a switch and soft Italian music drifted in the background. She was wowed. She couldn't believe he'd gone to all this trouble.

'You've done a good job,' she said appreciatively.

He handed her a wine glass. 'The good news is I'm assured this is an excellent wine, but you only get to drink two glasses.'

Ivy leaned forward and ran her finger down the condensation on the wine bottle. She couldn't help but smile. 'This is perfect,' she whispered.

Travis gestured towards the bench seat. 'So, let's imagine we're back at Gino's. I've bought us drinks and I'm sitting, waiting for you to arrive.' He gave her a sexy smile. 'And now here you are. Walking through the door and making me pinch myself with how lucky I feel right now.'

Ivy watched as he poured the wine into the glass and handed it to her. She sat down next to him, feeling the heat emanating from his body towards her.

She crossed her legs and held up her glass of wine. 'Okay, so how are we doing this? Are we doing a completely new date? Me as Ali and you as Rob? Or are we skipping to the part where we're Ivy and Travis?'

He opened one of the beer bottles and held it up, chinking it against her glass. 'How about we agree to skip to the good part?'

She leaned one elbow on the table. 'Let me think about that. It's been…' she glanced up through hooded lids '…six long, long days. We've done the introductions. We've stumbled through the getting-to-know-you part.'

He lifted his eyebrows as if he was wondering where this was going.

Her heart was racing in her chest. She knew

she was about to throw caution completely to the wind. Her career could literally hang in this guy's hands if they argued at a later date. But in her head she was separating the two parts of their lives—personal and professional.

'We have the forty-five-day reprieve of having two drinks tonight. And…' she leaned over and surveyed the bar snacks '…we have chicken wings, steak fries, peanuts, chips and olives.' She leaned towards him and said in a low voice, 'Why, Travis, I think we might have struck gold.'

She'd only managed the barest sip of her wine before his lips were on hers.

'You know what?' he murmured. 'I think you might be right.'

The paper on the walls was fragile and ended up scattered over the floor. Ivy laughed when she stretched out a few hours later after falling asleep. There was no way this room would meet any kind of regulations if someone were to walk in.

She blinked as she wondered what had woken her up, thankful that something had because she really needed to get back to her own cabin. The last thing she wanted to do on an aircraft carrier was to be caught sneaking back to her cabin. Her dress was in a crumpled heap on the floor, alongside her shoes, and she swung her legs out of bed to make a grab for them.

There was a noise beside her. Then a grunt. She'd only just repositioned her underwear before she realised what was happening.

Travis was definitely a restless sleeper. But as she dropped her dress over her head and tugged it into place she realised this was something entirely different. He was murmuring, his head starting to thrash from side to side.

'No, not that way. This way. Keep your head down. Cover your mouth.'

His arms and legs started to thrash too. 'Leave it!' he yelled, and she jumped in shock.

He was having a nightmare. Travis King was having a nightmare. For the first time in her medical career Ivy wasn't quite sure what to do. She'd never dealt with anyone having nightmares before. She'd heard a few friends talk about their kids having night terrors, but she couldn't remember what she should do. Did she wake him up? Or did she let it come to a natural end?

Inwardly she groaned. If Travis made much more noise, someone would surely come by to check on him. The last thing she wanted was for them both to be reported to the captain. She might as well kiss any chance of being SMO goodbye if that were to happen. No, she needed to deal with this the best way she could. For both their sakes. She hesitated next to his bed as Travis continued to thrash his legs and arms.

'No, not that way. Here, let me help you.' He started coughing—choking almost. Whatever this dream was, it was very real for Travis.

'Travis,' she said tentatively to begin with.

Nothing. He kept murmuring and thrashing.

She tried again, raising her voice a little. 'Travis, wake up.'

Still nothing. She bent forward and gently touched his arm. 'Travis, wake up.'

It was as if she hadn't even spoken. He just kept writhing in the bed, muttering under his breath. Before she even had a chance to think or move, *'No!'* he yelled at the top of his voice, his strong right arm lashing out and sending her back into the nearby bulkhead.

The noise must have disturbed him and touch must have registered with him because almost instantly he sat up, breathing fast and hard, eyes wide.

She stood frozen against the bulkhead, her arm across her chest. He hadn't hurt her in any way—she'd had worse shoves from people in the grocery store—but it was the element of surprise that took her breath away.

Travis's eyes were wide. 'Ivy?' It took him a few moments to reorientate himself. She could almost see him making sense of why she was in his cabin.

Her heart was thudding in her chest.

'Y-you…you…' she stammered, 'were having a nightmare.'

The look of horror on his face told her everything she needed to know. What she actually wanted to do was grab her shoes and jacket and get out of his cabin and back to her own, where she could make sense of it all.

But the doctor in her knew she shouldn't walk away. While she might not understand nightmares, she could understand trauma from a million miles away. Working in the armed forces meant she saw it in many forms, time and time again. She just hadn't expected it from Travis.

She took a few deep breaths, trying to let her heart rate return to normal and stop hammering away in her chest.

'Ivy, did I hurt you?' He was on his feet, stepping too close.

She flinched and she saw the pain in his eyes as he noticed and stepped back again.

She picked up the nearby chair that she must have stumbled over on her way back to the bulkhead. She pulled her dress straight and sat down, facing Travis.

'You didn't hurt me,' she said steadily. Then she took another breath. 'But you could have.'

He slumped down onto the bed. He looked as if she'd punched him in the guts.

'Travis, why don't you tell me what's going on?'

He leaned forward and put his head in his hands. She wanted to hug him. But she had to stay clear. She had to give him the space he needed to sort all this out in his head. She knew that she would need the same time later.

When he lifted his blue eyes to hers they were glistening with unshed tears. That was the moment that almost completely undid her. She tried to stay calm and rational. 'Travis, how long have you had nightmares like this?' Part of her brain shifted. This wasn't about her at all. It was about Travis. She had to treat him like a patient, not a lover. It was the only way she would be of any use to him.

His answer was throaty. 'Four years.'

'What happened four years ago?' There was no point in beating around the bush—not with a guy that a short time ago she'd been in an entirely different position with. She needed some honesty. But part of her brain stuck on the part that this had been happening to Travis for four years,

He ran his fingers through his hair. His voice shook as he spoke. 'Four years ago I was on deployment with a team that came under mortar fire. Three of my colleagues were killed instantly. Twenty were injured around me.'

She drew in a breath. She didn't need to ask where he'd been deployed. She'd spent a spell there too.

But Travis hadn't finished speaking. 'We were held down under gunfire for three days. I had limited resources and had to choose who to prioritise and who I could actually save.' He looked her in the eye. 'I relive that day every other night.'

She'd been lucky enough never to have come under direct fire, but as a surgeon in the area she'd dealt with the direct consequences of everyone else who had done. She could easily imagine the horrors of the experience.

Her skin prickled but something about what he'd said just didn't feel quite right. The words that he'd been using, the instructions he'd been shouting, had sounded more like a retreat than a lockdown.

'Is there anything else?' she probed.

He groaned, leaning back and wrapping his arms across his chest. His eyes fixed on a corner of the cabin. 'I thought I'd managed to get through things. I thought I'd got out okay. But a few months later I went to a conference at a hotel in Chicago. There was a fire in the middle of the night. The sprinkler system didn't work. Smoke was everywhere and I was on the thirtieth floor.'

These words made sense to her. The coughing and choking he'd been doing during his nightmare, the instruction he'd been shouting.

'But you got out okay?'

He gave a wry laugh as he shook his head. 'It's amazing, isn't it? The number of people who stay in a hotel and actually don't look for the fire stairs, even though they know they should? I banged on all the doors on my floor and helped everyone to the stairs. But I had to stop at every floor, yelling to others so they could actually find the escape route. On a couple of floors I found people already suffering from smoke inhalation.'

'So you stopped to help?' She knew as soon as she asked the question that he had.

He gave a horrid shiver. 'The smoke was particularly bad on some floors. I tried to check them all, but afterwards I found out that I had missed a few people already overcome.'

She could see that he blamed himself, even though there was no reason to.

He kept talking and as he lifted one arm she noticed a little puckering on the skin towards the back. Her fingers hadn't noticed that spot in her earlier exploration.

'Travis, were you physically hurt in either the mortar attack or the fire?'

She could see every muscle in his body tense. 'Barely.'

'What does that mean?'

He stood up and turned around. Under one shoulder blade was an area that had clearly been burned. The same on the top side of his left upper arm. Scattered across the base of his spine were some small areas that looked like some kind of shrapnel.

She had missed them all. She'd been to bed with a man with war wounds and burns and she'd missed them all. It seemed illogical to her but as her mind relived the previous few hours, she realised her hands had mainly been around his neck, on his face, in the middle of his back or other places.

'I'm sorry,' she said simply.

Travis was back on his feet, then kneeling before her. 'No, I'm sorry, Ivy. I never meant to hurt you. I never meant to scare you.'

She knew that. She knew all of that. But there was something more important here. 'Sit down.'

Her tone was sterner than she wanted it to be, but the best way she could help Travis right now was to keep down this path.

'Anything we talk about in this cabin doesn't leave this cabin, you understand?'

He nodded and she could see his expression change. He'd realised she'd stopped looking at him like a lover and had started looking at him as a patient.

'Travis, what just happened when we were in bed together—has this ever happened before?'

He shook his head.

She furrowed her brow. 'You're telling me that at no point in the last four years you've slept in a bed with another woman?' She gave a wry laugh. 'I don't expect you to have been a saint, Travis.'

He cringed a little and gave her an answer without looking at her. 'Of course I've slept with other women, but I've never stayed the night. I've never actually fallen asleep or spent the night with a woman in the last four years.'

'Oh.' It was the only thing she could think of to say right now. Travis had fallen asleep with her. *Her.* The first woman in four years he'd been comfortable enough with to fall asleep with. What did that mean?

'And the reason you haven't stayed overnight with a woman for the last four years?'

He took a deep breath and she let her question hang in the air. She knew the answer to that. He didn't want to admit what the problem was. He didn't want to face up to it. Maybe he hadn't accepted he had PTSD? Maybe he just wanted to keep it secret. But right now it was the biggest problem in this cabin. Travis King was in denial. And she couldn't pretend it wasn't breaking her heart.

She took a deep breath. 'Travis. I don't need to spell this out. You need help. You must know you need help. Have you done anything about this?'

The words hung in the air between them and again he didn't answer—which was all the answer she needed.

Anger surged through her. She wanted to help him—she did. But he had to want to help himself first.

He opened his mouth to speak but no words actually came out.

Ivy stood up. 'Travis, I would like to see if this relationship has a chance. I think we could be good together. But I can't help you if you don't want to help yourself. I think the best thing I can do right now is give you some space to get some help.' She gave a sad sigh.

'And even though I'm a doctor, this isn't my area of speciality. I'm not sure that I'm the best person to help you right now, but if you need me, you know where to find me. All you have to do is ask.'

Her voice trembled as she reached out and hugged him, feeling his warm body next to hers. Part of her wanted to stay in this position. But that wouldn't help Travis—not in the long term. If he remained in denial, he would suffer like this for the rest of his life. And she truly didn't want that for him.

Tears were pooling in her eyes and she knew she had to get out of here. If he liked her as much as she liked him, she could only pray that he would reach out for help. And if he did, she would absolutely be there.

'Let me know,' she said quietly before she broke down completely. And with that Ivy picked up her shoes and jacket and walked out the door.

CHAPTER EIGHT

HE WAS LIVING his life on autopilot and could barely look at Ivy right now.

This was all his fault. Everything she'd said to him had been fair and reasonable. She was right to walk away. All he could feel was shame and humiliation that whilst he'd been in the middle of a nightmare he might have accidentally hurt her.

But the part that had killed him most was when he'd seen the change in her eyes. When she'd started looking at him like a patient rather than the man she'd just made love with. He didn't ever want Ivy to look at him like that. He'd revealed a part of himself that he'd never shared with another, and she'd automatically gone into doctor mode.

Would he have done the same if the situation were reversed? Trouble was, he wasn't entirely sure.

Once or twice he'd thought about trying to

talk to her, maybe even texting her. But how could he talk to her when he hadn't sorted himself out?

Aileen had caught him looking at Ivy a few times and raised her eyebrows in a question. He knew Aileen would be happy for him to take her up on the offer that she'd made, but as soon as he had that conversation then it was there, on his record, forever.

If he were having this conversation with any of his friends, he would tell them not to be ridiculous. He would tell them the diagnosis wouldn't matter, that getting treatment was far more important. And he knew all that. But he also knew how the navy worked. Would he ever get another commission as an SMO with PTSD in his medical records? That was the harsh reality he was facing.

It was why he'd spent the last four years trying to pretend this wasn't actually happening to him.

Aston, one of the medical corpsman, came and tapped him on the shoulder. 'Dr King, I've got a female patient who needs to see a doctor. She's asking specifically for Dr Ross, but she's off duty. Should I go and find her?'

Travis shook his head. 'Ivy was on duty last night and had a tough case. I'll speak to the patient in the first instance. If I need to, I'll go and find Ivy.'

The medical corpsman handed over the notes. 'Room Two.'

Travis nodded and scanned them quickly. They were brief. He headed into Room Two and the young woman turned to look at him.

He gave her a smile as he sat down. 'I'm Dr King. I know you're looking for Dr Ross, but she's just gone off shift and I imagine she's sleeping right now. If it's okay with you, I can take some details and arrange for Dr Ross to see you later or some time tomorrow? I just wanted to see you to check if you need any emergency treatment.' He didn't want anything urgent for this patient to be overlooked, wanted to make sure it was safe to allow her to wait.

'Are you happy to chat with me?'

She gave a nervous nod.

'I'm Rena,' she said. 'I just wanted to see an actual doctor rather than a corpsman.'

'No problem,' said Travis. 'I'm happy to see you, but know that our medical corpsmen are fully trained.'

She didn't say anything so he continued, 'Can you tell me what brings you here today?'

She pressed her lips together. 'I just feel really tired. I can't get out of my bed in the morning, and I don't want to eat. As soon as I've finished my duties I just want to go back to bed.' She gave a laugh. 'I couldn't even drink my designated alcohol the other night. Just the smell of it…' She shuddered.

Travis gave a nod and took some notes. This could be a wide variety of conditions. He asked a few more questions. After a few minutes he started to sense where this might be going.

'Rena, how long have you been on board?'

'Since we started. It would be…twelve weeks now.'

Travis gave a nod. 'Do you mind if we run through a list of other symptoms?'

She shook her head.

'Okay, any abdominal pain?'

Her face twisted and she gave a half nod. 'Maybe a little. I just thought it was menstrual cramps. But it's a bit sharper than what it's normally like.'

Travis nodded. 'Indigestion? Nausea? Light-headedness? Headaches? Or palpitations?'

She shook her head at some and nodded at others.

'Do you mind if I ask you for a urine sample too? I'd like to rule out a urine infection.' He handed her a sample dish and Rena headed to the toilet. He wondered if he should actually go and wake up Ivy. He had a sneaky suspicion he might know what was wrong with Rena.

He stuck his head out the door and gave a shout to one of the other staff. 'Can you ask Ivy to come along? And apologise for waking her up. I want to do an abdominal scan on this young woman and think she might be happier if Ivy did that.'

Five minutes later Travis was in the treatment room, testing the urine sample.

'You called?' Ivy was rubbing her eyes. Her hair was rumpled and she was wearing scrubs that she'd clearly been sleeping in.

He gave a nod. 'I'm sorry to wake you up.'

She shook her head and stepped forward. 'No probs. Who is the patient?'

He turned the tablet around so she could read his notes. After a minute she looked up and glanced at the test strips. She gave a sigh. 'Okay, so I'm betting there's no infection, is there?'

He shook his head.

'Did you do the other test?'

He turned the pregnancy test around and she gave an even bigger sigh.

'How bad is her abdominal pain?'

'Right now it's just starting. She described as being like menstrual cramps, only sharper.'

Ivy didn't miss a beat. 'And if this pregnancy is ectopic, it's about to get a whole lot worse.' She nodded her head and paused before meeting his gaze. 'I was going to be cranky. But you were right to wake me. I'll do her ultrasound and have the conversation.'

As he nodded and turned to leave she called him back. 'Travis, you know how I hadn't delivered a baby in years?'

'Yes?'

'Well, it's been just as long since I dealt with an ectopic pregnancy. I'd feel happier if you'd scrub in too.'

A warm feeling spread across him. He knew what it was costing her to say those words out loud. No surgeon wanted to admit that something wasn't really their speciality. 'Would you like me to do the surgery?'

She shook her head. 'No, I'll do it. But I would appreciate if you stayed in case I have any questions.'

'No problem.'

She bit her lip. 'You do realise there's another issue here, don't you?'

Travis met her gaze. 'Of course. Ectopic pregnancies happen at around six weeks and we've been at sea for twelve, meaning Rena's got pregnant while she's been on board.'

Ivy's gaze dropped to the screen again. 'We all know the rules. I'm not entirely sure I feel comfortable getting a young woman into trouble for an act we both engaged in ourselves.'

Her straight talking reminded him just why he liked her so much. Ivy wasn't shy. She got right to the point. He couldn't help but smile at her. 'I guess you're right, but one of us will still need to have that conversation with her at a later date. We also need to think about contraceptive advice for her.'

Ivy leaned against the bulkhead for a minute. 'This is a tricky one. If the ultrasound confirms what we suspect, she'll need surgery. While I'm doing the ultrasound, could you ask Aileen if she might be available to counsel Rena later? I'm not sure how she'll react to the news about the pregnancy being ectopic.'

For the briefest of moments he paused as he felt a tiny moment of dread circle around him at the thought of talking to Aileen. He immediately shook it off. 'Of course I will. I'll meet you back here.'

Aileen was working in one of the other offices and gave him a wide smile as he knocked on the door. 'Travis, what can I do for you? Do you need my help?'

The look of expectation in her eyes made him want to cringe. 'Yes,' he said quickly. 'We have a young woman who probably has an ectopic pregnancy. We're not quite sure how she'll take the news and Ivy wondered if you'd be available if required.'

'Oh.' For a moment he thought she looked a bit disappointed. 'Of course, no problem at all. Eh... Travis? Anything else?'

He could say something. He could say it right now. Admit that something was wrong and that he needed help. The words were almost there, on the tip of his tongue, but...they just wouldn't go any further. He gave Aileen his best bright smile. 'No, that's great, thanks.'

As he walked back outside he thought he'd feel relief. But instead it was as if a baby whale had taken a spot on his shoulders and was pressing down. Hard.

He couldn't let this go on. Ivy had clearly been avoiding him these last few days, but just one glimpse of her, one whiff of her perfume, had made him realise how much he was allowing all this to hold him back—to steal part of the life that he really wanted.

A life with Ivy.

The impulse to lie down on the nearest bed and go back to sleep was slowly diminishing. Rena was a nice young girl who hadn't even asked Ivy any questions when she'd asked if she could do an ultrasound. The scan quickly told Ivy what she needed to know. She put the transducer back in its holder and turned to Rena. 'Okay, we need to talk about what happens next.'

'Am I pregnant?' Rena winced a little as she moved on the bed.

Ivy nodded. 'You are pregnant, but this pregnancy is unusual. The egg hasn't implanted in the lining of your womb.'

'It hasn't? What's wrong? Is that why I'm so uncomfortable?'

Ivy nodded and took the time to explain. There was a good chance that the general discomfort that Rena was feeling would rapidly increase. They had to operate as soon as possible. Ivy spoke slowly. 'Rena, is there anyone on board you would like me to get for you? A friend? A colleague? I think it's important you have someone to support you.'

She saw Rena waver before she shook her head. Maybe the pregnancy was a surprise. Somewhere on board this vessel was a man who'd shared a few intimate moments with Rena. Or it could be something else.

Ivy paused. Sexual assault wasn't unknown on military vessels. She bent forward and took Rena's hand, giving it a light squeeze. 'Rena, is there anything you need to tell me? As Flight Surgeon I'm responsible for making sure you feel safe on the *Coolidge*. I want you to know that you can tell me anything.'

A flash of recognition sparked in Rena's eyes and she shook her head. 'No, nothing like that. You don't need to worry about me.' Then her expression changed, and she laid her hand on her belly. 'So, all of this will be over once I've had the op?'

Ivy nodded. 'We'll take you in very soon. The last thing we want is for your pain to worsen and the ectopic pregnancy to rupture.'

'But you still need to take the tube away?'

'Yes, we do. There's no other way.'

'And I'll still be able to have children in the future?'

Ivy nodded. 'You should do. You have two fallopian tubes. I'll refer you to an ob-gyn specialist that you can see once we're back on land. They'll be able to run some tests and reassure you.'

Rena gave a nod, but her eyes had a distant kind of expression.

'One of the nurses will be in to get you ready for Theatre. I'll see you in there,' said Ivy.

She walked through the door and started as she saw Travis waiting for her. 'You were good with her,' he said, giving a small nod in appreciation.

Ivy's first instinct was to brush him off. As

far as she was aware, he still hadn't done what she'd asked but, then, she would never really know unless he told her.

He certainly hadn't asked her for help. But maybe he felt that wasn't appropriate. And she wasn't offended, really, more frustrated. She just wanted Travis to admit what was wrong and start the process of getting help.

She couldn't deny that, no matter what else happened, she liked Travis. He was a good guy. A good guy with a condition that needed to be treated. No matter how much she wanted to help, the first step, the denial part, Travis had to deal with himself.

She had experience of being around people who wouldn't help themselves in the first instance. One of her friends, Joss, back in university days, had Type One diabetes. Joss had continually ignored her blood-sugar results, her hypoglycaemic attacks and her secondary symptoms. Ivy had bent over backwards to help Joss, intervening on countless occasions, spending hours and hours with her friend when she had been sick, almost failing one exam in the process.

She'd finally realised that she couldn't do it for Joss. Joss had to do it for herself, and she'd slowly backed away. She'd heard later that a few years down the line Joss had self-destructed and had crashed her car while driving with low blood sugar. Luckily, Joss hadn't injured anyone else, just herself, and it had given her the wake-up call she'd needed.

Even though she was a doctor, Ivy couldn't always 'fix' someone. They had to want to 'fix' themselves. And as hard as it was to know how much Travis was hurting, he'd already been on this road for the last four years—and hadn't done anything about it. She knew how it would feel if she tried to intervene. She couldn't take sleepless nights and countless arguments—or the fear of him lashing out in his sleep again. As his blue eyes fixed on hers in the shadow of the corridor, she remembered the feel of his skin next to hers. There was so much about this guy she could actually love. There was so much potential between them. It actually felt as if she could reach out and grab it.

Deep down she knew it wasn't the way to start a relationship. But that didn't mean she couldn't be friends with him. Maybe that was what he needed most.

She gave him a smile. 'Well, I try my best.'

'I'm sorry I got you up. I heard you had a bad night.'

'I've had worse.' The words were out before she had a chance to think about them. Of course she hadn't been referring to her night with Travis. She had been thinking back to her many night shifts as an intern. But for the briefest of seconds she saw the wounded expression on his face. She couldn't leave it. She just couldn't.

Ivy reached out and put her hand on his arm. 'I didn't mean that.' She glanced over her shoulder to make sure no one could hear. 'Part of that night was very nice, as you know, and I appreciate the effort you made.'

She was trying to keep her tone light. She was just about to go into surgery with this guy and she needed them both to be on the same page.

He gave a silent nod and she tried to move on. 'Are you ready to be my wingman?'

That made his eyebrows lift in amusement. 'I'm your wingman? I don't get to be top gun?'

She shook her head. 'Oh, no, you're the wingman, absolutely. No one gets to be top gun in my theatre but me.'

'Fair enough. I'm happy to be your wingman.'

She was surprised by that. Most surgeons would never concede to another, particularly if they were senior. 'Let's go.' He nodded as the anaesthetic nurse slipped into Rena's room.

* * *

Surgery went smoothly. Whilst Ivy hoped she'd always be able to cope with any surgical emergency, it gave her confidence knowing there was someone else who could step in to help if required. They bantered easily, and she could see a number of staff exchanging glances above their masks. Ivy talked out loud, listing what she was doing and what she could see. It was what she would normally do when teaching students, but she was just outlining everything to reassure herself, and allowing Travis to add anything he felt she might have missed.

When she'd closed he stripped off his theatre garb and put his hand on her shoulder. 'Well done. Textbook case.'

And she felt it. That connection again, even though she had a theatre gown and scrubs between his skin and hers.

'Thanks for the support,' she said simply. 'It's appreciated.'

The nurse anaesthetist released the brakes on the trolley to push Rena to the post-op room. 'I can take over here and monitor our patient.' She glanced at the clock. 'Hurry on up, you two, before the mess stops serving.'

Ivy turned instantly. 'Oh, no, you go, Ellen. Grab some dinner while you can.'

Ellen shook her head. 'I have a green kale

smoothie. New diet, folks. Go and live the dream for me and eat some real food.' She rolled her eyes, laughing as she pushed Rena through to the next room.

It seemed awkward to refuse to go and eat together when there wasn't much time left. Travis held the door while Ivy stripped off her theatre gown and washed her hands again. 'Shall we?'

She nodded as they walked down the corridor, ignoring the fact that she could smell his aftershave. The mess was half-empty and they grabbed what was left on offer and sat down at a table. Most of the staff from the medical department had already eaten dinner and left, so there was no one to cushion their conversation.

He waited until they'd sat down before he spoke. 'I'll sort things. I will.'

She held her breath, waiting for him to continue.

'How do you feel about waiting?'

The question blindsided her. 'W-waiting?' she stuttered.

He nodded. 'Yup, waiting. How do you feel about it?'

A whole wave of emotions swept over her. She turned her eyes to meet his. 'What exactly do you mean by waiting?' Her skin prickled at his words.

His voice was low and throaty. 'I mean, is that something you would even consider? I like you, Ivy. You know I do. Our connection feels real. It felt real even before we met, and now? Even more so.' His fork pushed his food around the plate. 'I like the thing that we've got going.' He corrected himself, 'Or *had* going. I'd like to see where it could take us. I'd like to hope that at some point we might actually have a future together.'

She felt frozen. She hadn't expected him to come out with that. They'd flirted, connected, and she'd had all the same hopes too. But was it realistic? Or were they just fooling each other this might actually have some potential.

The tick-tick of her career potential was still ticking loudly in her head. There was still so much she wanted to achieve. Would she still be able to focus her time and energy on that, as well as committing to a relationship?

Despite her words a week ago, she did still have that little piece of her heart hoping. Travis had seemed like he might actually be perfect for her. She'd spent her last few years avoiding any relationship entanglements. Could she really be contemplating one now? It was a huge leap for her. But she got the impression it might be a leap for him too.

'I haven't fallen asleep with a woman for the

last four years. I haven't been relaxed enough to do so. But my nightmares and flashbacks have also never been so bad.'

'You're blaming me?' she asked with her hand on her chest.

He shook his head fiercely. 'No, of course not.' He set down his cutlery and put his hand on his own chest. 'I'm blaming me. Not you. You're the first person I've been relaxed around. The first person I've felt a real connection with, and the first person I've opened up to.'

She couldn't breathe. They were sitting in a half-filled mess hall with chatter and laughter all around them, but all she could concentrate on was him.

He spoke again. 'You're the first person who's made me stop and question if I'm sick.'

She knew how big those words were. She knew how much they meant.

Deep down, Ivy understood that Travis had never said those words out loud before. He was finally admitting he'd been in denial.

So she went with her heart instead of her head.

She moved her hand across the table and intertwined her fingers with his. 'I'm glad you want this, Travis. But you have to be sure you want this for you, not for me. You have to want to fix yourself.'

He nodded. 'I do. I really do. And I understand you might not want to wait around for that—because I've no idea how long that might take, or if I can even do it.'

It was those words that tore at her heartstrings—that convinced her his motivations were good. The *I* word. It was the one she'd wanted to hear.

She gave him a small smile as she squeezed her fingers in his. 'I think you might be worth waiting for,' she replied in a small whisper.

CHAPTER NINE

THE LOW-LEVEL SIREN sounded in the middle of the night and Travis sat bolt upright. For a moment he was back on the ground behind a wall as shots were being fired around him. It only took him a moment to gather himself before he was on his feet and out into the corridor.

He marched quickly to the sick bay. 'What's happening?'

One of the medical corpsman was grabbing some equipment. 'We stopped to assist a US vessel with engine trouble. But apparently some of the crew are sick.' He looked at Travis and shook his head. 'I'm sure we'll be able to cope. From what I hear, it doesn't sound too serious.'

There was a groan nearby. Travis moved into the ward area. There was an unfamiliar face curled up in one of the beds.

Jan, one of the nurses, gave him a nod. 'Abdominal pain,' she said. 'Just waiting for the ultrasound machine.'

'Any other symptoms?'

She shook her head. 'Not yet. He came in with cramps a few hours ago. We've taken some bloods.'

Travis gave a nod just as the man sat upright in bed and vomited everywhere. Both he and Jan jumped back, then exchanged glances. A few of the other staff scurried over and donned gloves and aprons.

'I know what happens next,' Travis murmured, as the man jumped from his bed.

'I need to use the bathroom,' the man said as he headed for the patient toilet.

'Lock down this area,' said Travis quickly. 'Is this one of the men from the rescued vessel—or is this one of our crew? He needs to be isolated in a single room and essentially barrier nursed right now.'

The staff moved quickly. They all knew exactly what this could mean for an aircraft carrier. Any kind of norovirus outbreak could be devastating for the working of the carrier.

'Jan, once the situation is under control we'll need an emergency meeting of the medical team. We need to control this situation.'

Tony came walking in behind him. 'There's

six of them—and they are all like him.' He nodded to the guy now back on the bed. 'He was sent up for pain relief. I did say to put him in a single room.' He sighed and shook his head and looked at Travis. 'Sorry.' Then he groaned. 'But we don't have six single rooms. We'll have to put them all together and term it a red zone.'

Travis looked at Tony. They both knew that staff could already have been infected by being in contact with any of the men from the ship. If he didn't get this under control...

One hour later his whole team was in front of him—including Ivy. She looked immaculate as usual, her hair tied back and clean blue scrubs in place.

'Hi, folks, we think we could have a potential outbreak of norovirus—or something similar. All six men from the vessel that was just rescued are potentially infected. Since we didn't know that when we initially rendered assistance, we now need to track, trace and isolate any members of our crew who have been in contact with them and monitor them over the next seventy-two hours. We all know the potential here. We have to try and contain this outbreak.'

Ivy exchanged a glance with him. 'Have you briefed the captain?'

He nodded and gave her a painful smile. 'Just back from doing that.'

She winced. She knew exactly how much of a rollicking any SMO would get while telling a captain that his ship with over five thousand crew could be carrying an infectious virus. He nodded at several of his staff. 'Everyone, full protective equipment while working with affected cases. Limited personnel in that ward. Report any development of symptoms.'

He took a deep breath. 'Okay, folks, there will be an investigation into why we allowed these men onto our vessel in the first place. I want you all to know that I support you. If we'd actually known what the problem was, we could have put some precautions in place. However, five of these men are clinically dehydrated—this seems a particularly ugly strain of norovirus—and we've already had to put them on IV fluids.'

'Do you want to break us into teams?'

Tony put his arm up straight away. 'I've already had contact. I'll continue to look after the patients.'

But Travis shook his head. 'No, you're our first case of isolation. You've been exposed and will likely develop the condition yourself.' He nodded to Ivy. 'You lead the track and trace team. Find all our personnel who had contact with the men on the vessel and find a space for them to spend the next few days.'

Ivy looked at a list on her lap and pulled a face. 'I've already started. Most of the personnel were from Engineering. They went on board to try and help with the breakdown.'

Travis held in a groan. 'Perfect. Captain will love that when I tell him.' He shook his head but held up his hands. 'It is what it is. Incubation is around forty-eight hours but can be longer. If our staff have no signs or symptoms, they can be released back to their normal stations after seventy-two hours. Until then they go nowhere. First sign of any symptoms, they get shipped up here. To me.'

Ivy frowned. 'You're going to staff the ward?'

He nodded, hands on his hips. 'I was here when the first guy started vomiting. I didn't have any direct contact like Tony. But…?' He held up his hands. 'Droplets. There is a chance I've already been exposed. It makes sense for me to continue to work in here, alongside the other staff, where we'll be wearing full PPE.'

Norovirus was the kind of disease that felled cruise ship passengers and meant that ships were refused docking in ports. Having an outbreak on board the *Coolidge* would be disastrous.

Travis handed her a piece of paper. 'I've sketched out a plan of how we might have to isolate people around the ship. We have provisions to make the medical bay larger if we have to.'

She took the paper from him, her hand brushing against his.

Regret flooded through him again. 'Ivy—'

She held up her hand. 'Work, Travis. Let's prioritise work right now. We can chat later.'

He gave a nod of his head. He understood exactly why she felt this way. And he knew he needed to address the problem. He'd been allowing worries about his career to stop him taking the next steps, but as he breathed in and caught the orange-scented shampoo that Ivy used, his career was the last thing on his mind.

His job didn't define who he was, or who he could be. He'd spent the last few years making excuses why relationships didn't really work out for him. Never allowing himself to fall asleep next to a woman was likely to be a huge factor. One that he'd been carefully ignoring. That wasn't a way to live. It wasn't a way to love.

And everything about Ivy made him feel like he was heading in that direction. The fact he'd fallen asleep next to her told him everything he needed to know. Even if his brain hadn't caught up with it yet, his body was telling him this was the woman he wanted to be around. He'd known straight away she was bringing up demons for him. But no one else could deal with those demons but him.

He'd even sent another few emails to his friend in San Diego about the private practice offer. Asking more questions, exploring the area more thoroughly, in a way he'd never really been motivated to before.

But it seemed that dealing with Ivy and his career contemplations would have to wait—for now.

'Okay, folks,' he said. 'Let's get to work.'

CHAPTER TEN

'HE ASKED YOU to do *what*?' Liz's disbelieving voice was shrill.

'Wait,' sighed Ivy. 'He asked me to wait.'

'And you said yes?' Her tone let Ivy know exactly what she thought of that.

Ivy was beyond tired. Tracking, tracing and isolating had led to some interesting discoveries about what the personnel on the ship really got up to. As a result, she now had one hundred staff isolated in special quarters. All they seemed to do was complain. It had been forty-eight hours and all she wanted to do was sleep. But she'd been dodging Liz's messages for the last few days until finally CALL ME NOW! had appeared on her phone screen.

'I thought something was wrong,' she said, and sighed as she sagged back down on her bed.

'Something *was* wrong. My best friend was deliberately ignoring me. You only do that when you've done something you know I won't approve of.' There was a tiny pause. 'I get you're at close quarters with this guy, but do you really think you know him well enough to make that kind of decision. It sounds kind of serious to me.'

'It sounds serious to me too,' Ivy admitted. 'But...' she shifted on her bed, uncomfortable '... I can't explain it. I just feel kind of connected to him, in a way I never have before.'

'Careful,' warned Liz. 'You sound as if you're getting kind of sappy. What happened to my own Boudicca? Mistress of all around her and heading for the top job? The girl who vowed she didn't have time for a relationship.'

That prickled. 'She's definitely still here,' said Ivy defensively. 'Just because I might like a guy, it doesn't mean he'll get in the way of my career.'

'Really?' Sarcasm dripped from Liz's voice. 'Because it sounds to me like Mr Wonderful has told you he's not all that wonderful and asked you to hang around until he feels better.'

Ivy tried to butt in, but Liz just kept on talking.

'And what if he never gets better, Ivy? Are you supposed to wait forever?'

'He hasn't asked me to do that at all. He just

asked me for some time to get some help, and then see how things go from there.'

'Girl, have you listened to yourself? While I get it that you're in a tiny space and feelings might be amplified because, for the first time in forever, there is a man with a hint of potential around you, what if you wait, and then finally get together, and the spark dies—like it does for a lot of romances? And you've wasted time and energy, and in the meantime your real Mr Wonderful has drifted on by?'

Ivy squeezed her eyes closed in frustration. 'But what if he's Mr Wonderful and I don't give him the chance to fulfil his role in my life?'

Liz gave the biggest sigh in the world. 'Oh, girl, you've got this *bad*.'

Ivy finally laughed. 'Let me assure you, I'm still focused on my job. I'm still chasing my dream. Travis will not get in the way of that. I wouldn't let him.' She rolled over onto her back and looked up at the grey ceiling. 'But can't a girl have a few dreams while she's waiting?'

'Sounds like you've made up your mind.'

'I have,' she admitted.

Liz was silent for a few moments and then she spoke again. 'I hope he's worth it, Ivy. I really do. Because the guy that gets you has to know just how special you are.'

Ivy knew Liz was only being protective. And she liked it. She was her best friend, and when she met Travis it was important to her that Liz and Travis liked each other.

'Thanks, honey. See you later.'

She'd barely finished the call when a text appeared on her phone.

Sleeping yet?

Travis. It was Travis. She glanced at the clock in her cabin. It was nearly 1:00 a.m. Whilst she might have been dying to snuggle up in bed, her brain had just been sparked awake again instantly.

She answered quickly.

Is there a problem on the ward?

No. Awake, but tired. Have a host of people around me, but miss you.

Her heart missed a few beats. Wow. When he wanted to be, this guy was good.

She didn't wait to reply. That was the thing about being sleepy. There wasn't time to craft answers. She didn't have the brain space for it right now.

You're still on the ward? Why aren't you in bed?

His reply took a little time to appear.

One of our staff has been infected. He's diabetic and we can't get him stabilised. Sliding scale and insulin/dextrose infusion isn't helping at all. Think I'll need to stay here all night.

She replied instantly.

You need to sleep. But maybe not in full view of everyone. I can come and take over if you like.

No way. Don't want you exposed to this.

Part of her felt warm and cosy about that response, but part of her wanted to do her job.

You can't treat me differently from anyone else and you can't be on duty twenty-four hours a day. Where's Tony?

As soon as she sent the message she could guess the response that would appear.

Man down. He had no PPE when he made first contact. He started vomiting a few hours ago.

He is NOT happy being in bed in the ward, but I insisted.

Ivy didn't want to laugh but she knew Tony well. He would be a hideous patient.

Are you okay?

Her screen filled with three dots. They seemed to hover there for a while as if he'd changed his mind, deleted his response and written something else.

Truthfully? Wishing I was anywhere but here... actually, wishing I was with you.

This guy could melt her heart for real. She sucked in a breath. She would love to be wrapped in Travis's arms right now, but no matter how good her imagination was, it couldn't be a reality. How could she relax enough to fall asleep with him when he could have another nightmare? Her heart felt as though it was twisting in her chest.

She tried not to think too much. She could send all that stuff in a text, but it felt like blaming, and she didn't want to do that. She didn't want to be the person who agreed to wait, and then at the first opportunity pushed it back in

his face because he hadn't worked to get better yet.

But it was as if he'd read her mind.

I'm going to speak to Aileen. She's the best
place for me to start. But starting the conversation feels...huge. Bigger than me.

She wanted to wrap her arms around him
in a huge hug. But before she got a chance the
little dots appeared again, followed by another
message.

You haven't answered, so not sure how things
are in your head. Sometimes I feel like a fraud.
We've both seen people affected by PTSD.
Some of them we know will never be the same
again because of their experiences. I'm so
aware that my experiences weren't as bad as
others. But the nightmares aren't going away,
and I've been purposely ignoring them, pushing them away so I don't have to deal with
them. But here, tonight, knowing that if I don't
do something we won't be able to fall asleep
in each other's arms kills me. Because it's all I
can think about. I don't want to be without you.

A tear slid down her cheek. For a moment
she thought about pinching herself to make

sure she hadn't fallen asleep and was actually dreaming all this.

Her fingers flew across her screen, all barriers well and truly lifted. He'd told her that he didn't want to be without her. It had been a long time since someone had said those words to her. Last time she'd doubted them. But this time, no matter what else was going on, she didn't doubt them for a second.

I want to be with you too. Don't doubt that. I want you to be well. I want to be able to curl up next to you and just listen to your breathing.

Her fingers hesitated. She wasn't ready to put her heart on the line until she was sure. Sure about everything. About where she was in her life, and if she was ready to lose her heart to someone.

Not someone. Travis.

She wondered if he might be disappointed with her reply. But within a heartbeat the little dots appeared.

A man can dream. I'll get there. I promise you. Sleep well. xx

She lay back and pressed her phone against her heart. Travis King didn't want to be without her. She wanted to dance around the cabin, but her body was just too tired. So she curled up, leaving her phone exactly where it was. She might not be able to cuddle up and feel the body of the man who was, without doubt, stealing a little part of her every day, but she could fall asleep with the words and messages that he was sending her. And, for now, that would have to be good enough.

CHAPTER ELEVEN

HE STARED AT Ivy's file again. He'd been asked
for a report. One part of him wanted to opt
out. He could hardly have an unbiased view of
Ivy and her work. But that was unheard of. It
would immediately raise red flags. Questions
would be asked. Her record would be blem-
ished by the fact her commanding officer had
asked someone else to write her report.

He might as well tell the world that something was going on between them.

It wasn't as if it had never happened in the
navy before. Plenty of colleagues had started
and maintained relationships together. As soon
as it had become known, they hadn't been allowed to serve together. It was part of the
rules—and rightly so. Relationship troubles
or marital debates couldn't be brought onto a
ship. And military decisions could be compro-
mised if a loved one was at stake.

That was why the navy kept things simple

and said that work and love had to be separate. This was probably the first time that Travis had completely understood why.

He stared at the blank screen. He knew exactly why he was being asked for a routine report on Ivy. This time it wasn't routine. An SMO vacancy was imminent, and she was one of the candidates up for consideration.

Her record was exemplary. Anyone who knew her would give her a report that reflected her skills and teamwork abilities. The glimmers of leadership that he'd already seen would flourish in this new role. Travis felt as if his heart was currently held in a vice. If he gave Ivy a glowing report—which she deserved— and someone pointed out the fact that there were rumours of a relationship between Travis and Ivy when he'd written said report, there was a chance it could damage both of their careers.

It weighed heavily on him. He was already in the position of SMO and unlikely to be given anything more than a sharp talk and a reminder to declare any relationship between serving personnel, whereas the repercussions could be much more serious for Ivy. It could move her from the top of the list—casting doubts on her true abilities and the final report he had written on her—and let someone else take the job that should be hers.

His head sagged into his hands. Any other man might just write Ivy a glowing report and send it in. But he knew how important this would be for her. Unfortunately everyday sexism still existed in the armed forces, and any whiff of rumour about Ivy could seriously damage her career. Travis would not be responsible for that.

He leaned back in his chair as Tony knocked on the door, bringing in some reports. Tony took one look at him. 'What's up?'

It was a light-bulb moment for Travis. 'Have a seat,' he said, gesturing to the chair in front of the desk.

Tony frowned for a moment. 'Is this where I ask what I've done?'

Travis shook his head and leaned forward. 'Tony, I know you're not a fool. I've been asked to write a recommendation about Ivy.'

Tony raised his eyebrows a little. 'And, of course, you will.'

Travis nodded. 'I will, but I'd like a little input from the team.'

The frown remained on Tony's face. 'That's not entirely normal. They usually only want to know what the boss thinks—particularly if it's going to be a recommendation about a promotion.'

Travis nodded in relief. Tony knew exactly what this was about. It made it easier.

'The last thing I want is to write the glowing recommendation that Ivy deserves and for anyone to cast shade on it because my feelings towards Ivy might not be…' He looked up at the ceiling. 'How do I say it? Not entirely unbiased?'

'But if you don't do it, that will be worse.'

'I know. But what if I did a collective response? Ivy's a team player. It's one of her best attributes. Not everyone who works with her has the same bias as me.'

Tony leaned back and folded his arms, looking thoughtful. 'So you want to use this different approach to make sure everyone says how great she is, not just you?'

Travis nodded. 'I'm not sure how many people know something is going on between Ivy and me—'

Tony let out a snort. 'Try half of the ship.'

Travis kept nodding. 'In that case, over two thousand people could cast aspersions when Ivy comes up for promotion.'

'Do you think anyone would actually do that? Ivy doesn't make enemies. She's a good doctor and a good officer.'

'I know that. But do I really know the mind-sets of two thousand people on this ship? The timing is awful. What I want to do is let Command know that Ivy and I are…' He paused, not quite sure what word to use.

'In a relationship,' said Tony for him.

Travis nodded and let out a long, slow breath from between his lips. Someone else saying the words out loud made it feel like a weight had been lifted from his shoulders.

'But if I do that now—just after they've asked for a recommendation—then it will instantly raise eyebrows.'

Tony leaned forward. 'And you don't want to do that. You don't want anyone to think about anything other than the fact that Ivy is worthy of promotion.'

'Exactly.'

Tony gave him a sideways look. 'It's an interesting approach.' He gave a slow nod. 'I'll ask a few key personnel if they'd like to write a contribution for Ivy's recommendation. Best not let everyone know. And I'll write one too.'

Travis gave a grateful nod. 'Thanks, Tony. I'll combine them all into one recommendation and send an email saying I thought a team approach might be a good idea for a change.' He screwed his face up. 'Maybe I'll pick some better words than that.'

Tony laughed. 'Yeah, whatever you do, don't make your recommendation look like a criticism of their process.'

Travis rolled his eyes. 'Nope. No way. I'm doing this to help her, not get in her way.'

Tony stood up, walked around and put his hand on Travis's shoulder. 'If you know her at all, you know how important this is to her. I appreciate you thinking about how to make this work best for her.' He gave another laugh. 'But you're right. Your timing does suck. Shoulda saved the loving for later!'

He was still laughing as he walked out the door.

Travis stayed in place for a few moments, his hands pressed down on the desk. He knew what he had to do next.

He'd found a kind of solution to support Ivy's promotion. As soon as that was completed he would need to talk to her to agree when they would let the powers above know that they were seeing each other. Or 'in a relationship', as the phrase went. That thought made him smile. It probably should worry him a little. But it didn't. He wanted to be able to say that. He wanted to be able to declare it to his colleagues and his friends.

It wasn't something he took lightly. An email flashed up on his screen. Peters again.

His emails were becoming a weekly obsession. Travis couldn't pretend it still wasn't a little flattering. He had to admit after the string of emails he was starting to become more open to a new role. And it was nothing to do with the potential income. Peters had mentioned the possibility of them being a healthcare provider for veterans. Travis liked that idea. He knew of lots of veterans who struggled with the healthcare system once their service was finished.

Ten years ago, he wouldn't have expected to consider that kind of career until he'd completed forty years of navy service. But things had changed for him. He was questioning more. He might not have openly accepted his PTSD before. But the fact that even before he'd taken this emergency SMO post he'd already been exchanging emails with Peters told him that, subliminally, his brain had already been trying to tell him things.

Travis shook his head. He wasn't in a position to think about private practice right now. He had to do something else first. He had to start his own treatment. Take the steps he should have taken four years ago.

He ignored the fact that his hands seemed to shake a little as he pressed them harder into the desk and stood. The walk down the corridor seemed to take an age.

People were nodding and saying hello as he passed, but his mind could only focus on one thing. He didn't want to allow himself the excuse of any interruptions.

He was doing this for himself. But he was also doing this in the hope for a new life. A life that meant he could wake up every morning next to the woman that he was starting to realise he might love.

When he reached the door he didn't hesitate, just gave a short knock and walked in.

Aileen looked up and gave him her normal warm smile. 'Hi, Travis, what can I do for you?'

He closed the door behind him and as he turned back again he noticed Aileen straighten a little in her chair. She knew. She knew what this was.

She gestured towards the chair next to her.

'Take a seat,' she said with a smile.

And he did.

CHAPTER TWELVE

IVY WAS FEELING ANTSY. It was the only way she could describe how she was feeling right now. And she couldn't quite put her finger on *why* she was feeling this way.

Travis had started treatment with Aileen for his PTSD. Only she and Aileen knew that. Ivy wasn't foolish. She knew this could be treatment that lasted a lifetime. But at least he'd taken the first step.

They'd also started seeing each other in as discreet a way as possible. Behind the closed doors of each other's cabins Ivy had learned all Travis's habits, likes and dislikes. She'd even seen his sisters through video chat, and loved the easy, teasing relationship all the siblings had. Travis was clearly the butt of many of their jokes. They'd also taken great pleasure in regaling her with embarrassing childhood tales of their brother, all at his expense.

Most of those calls ended with Travis shaking his head and cutting the connection to his hysterical sisters. But what was clearest to Ivy was the love and affection between the siblings. It reminded her of her own relationship with her sister and brother, Neil, who had asked Travis a million questions during one of their video calls as if he were interviewing him for a job. Finally, grudgingly, Neil had conceded to Ivy that he thought Travis might be 'okay'.

It was early evening and Ivy was leaning back against Travis as they watched a streamed talk show. It was ridiculous—one guest claimed he could see ghosts, a minor celeb was on her fifth marriage and a reality TV star was peddling her latest diet, which she claimed had helped lose her half her body weight.

Travis groaned. 'Why are we watching this mindless crap?' He was twiddling a strand of her hair in one of his fingers.

'Because I've done three minor surgeries today and seen another thirty patients, and now my brain can only compute "mindless crap", as you put it.'

Travis's warm hand slid over hers and rested on her belly. 'I can't convince you to watch a good eighties movie? *Ferris Bueller*? *The Lost Boys*? *Gremlins*?'

She laughed. 'I'm more a *Working Girl*, *Pretty in Pink* and *Mystic Pizza* kind of gal.'

He winced. 'We've missed the most obvious one, you do realise that, don't you?'

She closed her eyes and sagged back against his chest. 'If I could count on one hand the number of references people make about me to *Top Gun*, I'd be a millionaire.'

'Me too.' He laughed.

Her phone beeped and she leaned over and grabbed it, shaking her head when she read the screen.

'What is it?' he asked.

'Just a stupid online game I've been playing with friends. People send random memes with statements that you need to answer. It's all about keeping in touch.'

'So what did today's say?'

She turned the screen around to reveal a large pink cloud with words in black.

What are you doing today? What were you doing a year ago today? What do you hope to be doing this time next year?

Liz had already replied.

Eating chocolate and drinking wine. Eating chocolate and drinking wine. Eating chocolate and drinking wine. Hey? Who says I'm not progressive!

Travis shifted a little. 'So, what's your reply going to be?'

'You don't want to know that,' said Ivy carelessly.

'Actually, I do.'

She gave him a curious stare over her shoulder then settled back against his chest, knowing that he could read her reply. 'Okay, then.' She started typing on the screen.

Surgeon on the Coolidge in the Pacific. Surgeon on the George H. W. Bush in the South China Seas. Hopefully SMO on a vessel somewhere in the middle of an ocean!

'Hey,' he said gently, sliding his hand over hers again before she pressed Send. 'That's all about your job, Ivy. Not about you.'

It hadn't even occurred to her and she froze for a second. He gave her a half-playful poke in the ribs. 'Your friends want to know about your life, not the navy's.'

She twisted her head again. 'But the navy *is*

my life. Just like it is yours. That's why we're both here.'

His blue eyes were twinkling. 'But it isn't. We're here because of some weird coincidence that we met online—and almost in real life. The navy didn't bring us together, we did that ourselves. This…' he held his arms wide open '…is just our playground for now. It's not the end point for us.'

Now she sat up and turned around to face him, legs curled under her, the things he was saying prickling in her brain. She looked down at her phone. 'You're right. It *is* all work related.' She hated that she hadn't noticed that herself. She hated that the thought hadn't even *occurred* to her. The response she'd given had been automatic.

She stared down at her phone again, her mouth feeling very dry. She deleted what she had written and looked up at Travis. 'If you were asked this question, what would you write?'

All of a sudden it seemed very important what his answer would be.

Travis didn't hesitate at all. 'Today I'm snuggled up with my blind-date girl.' He winked at her. 'You can bet I'll be giving that app a five-star rating. Last year…' He looked up at the corner of the cabin as if he was trying to remember the date. 'I think I was home in San Diego, probably drinking in a bar somewhere with one of my crazy sisters. And this time next year?' His blue eyes connected with hers and he lowered his voice. 'I very much hope I'll be snuggled up in bed with you.'

Ivy tried to just breathe. She wanted to cry. She wanted to book herself into therapy somewhere. When had she started to focus her whole life on her career—when had that become everything to her?

As she sat for a few moments she couldn't actually pinpoint when it had happened. Had it always actually been like this? She'd wanted to be an SMO for as long as she could remember. It had always been her long-term career goal. It had felt good to aim for a top position. For the first time she was questioning herself. Had she put her career above everything else in an attempt to feel 'good enough'?

Or was it really the first time? Had the whole road down this path—using the app, thinking about a personal life, wondering if she might like to actually meet someone—been her mind's way of telling her to think about herself? Broaden her horizons, take some time to look at her emotional needs instead of focusing on her career goals.

Travis leaned forward and touched her arm.

'Ivy? What's wrong? I'm sorry. Did I scare you with my plans? I didn't mean to.' He stood up from her bed. 'I didn't mean to jump to any conclusions. I'm not trying to push you into anything…'

He was starting to babble and she shook her head, blinking back a few tears. 'No,' she said, shaking her head. 'It's not what you said…' She took a deep breath. 'Well, yes, it is. But I'm not scared, Travis. You're not jumping to conclusions. It's just the fact that your answers to the questions were so different from mine.' She put her hand up to her heart. 'And now you've got me thinking what kind of terrible person I am that when I get asked a casual question, my response is all about work.' Her voice was starting to shake.

Her phone pinged again as another friend responded and Ivy gave a small laugh and turned it around.

Growing a baby. Marrying the man I love. Probably having a million sleepless nights and probably relying on all my friends to assist!

Her friend was pregnant. Cassy, a mutual friend of Liz and herself, had just let them all know she was expecting. Now that definitely made a tear roll down her cheek. Cassy had a high-flying career at a bank in San Diego, but nowhere in her response had she mentioned it. Her response was all about family life.

'Hey...' Travis moved forward and pulled Ivy up towards him, wrapping his arms around her and holding her close. 'I'm sorry. Don't take this so seriously. I'm sure your friends just thought of this as a piece of fun.'

But those words just made the sob that had been stifled in her throat erupt. Her head was buried against Travis's chest. 'But what kind of a person am I? My first reaction was all about work.' She sniffed and looked up at him with blurred vision. 'You didn't do that, Travis. Why did I?'

Travis shook his head. 'Don't do this.' His fingers went under her chin and tilted it even more towards him. 'You are a wonderful surgeon. A brilliant team player. And a fabulous human being. Ask me what I think? I'm the man that's laying my heart at your feet.'

Ivy breathed. Trying to stem the flow of panic that she felt. Her hands gripped Travis's arms. 'Give me a second,' she said, picking up her phone and tapping the screen.

On a cruise with my blind date. Living a lonely but busy life. Hopefully cuddled up with the

man of my dreams. PS Congratulations Cassy—
will video call you later!

She pressed Send. The words were there.
But she still felt like a failure.

'Here.' She forced a smile onto her face as
she turned it towards him.

Travis only gave a brief nod. She was making this worse.

Ivy sat down on the edge of her bed. 'Why
don't you tell me how things are going with
Aileen?'

Something flitted across his face. Annoy-
ance? Maybe he didn't like the intrusion. Or
maybe he knew she was just trying to divert
attention from herself.

She saw him choose his words carefully.
'Things are going…fine. I think. I don't really know. I'm still having nightmares. But
Aileen's told me not to expect any kind of instant fix. She's also told me there's a chance
they might never totally go away.'

Oh, no. The expression on Travis's face
told her everything she needed to know. She
shouldn't have asked.

'Don't worry,' he said softly. 'I wouldn't ask
you to be with me if that happens. If you can't
feel safe around me, we can't be together.'

The look he gave her was the saddest she'd

ever seen. He ran a soft finger down her cheek. 'Goodnight, Ivy,' he said, and before she had a chance to say anything else he slipped out of the door.

Ice poured over her heart. She'd ruined a perfect evening by being nosy, being intrusive, because Travis's selfless answers had made her take a long hard look at herself. How much was she prepared to put into this relationship?

She'd drawn a line in the sand immediately with Travis and had sealed her heart into a package, right about the same time he'd started wearing his on his sleeve.

In her head she still had him as her potential dream date. She didn't have him in her head as Travis, the real-life person and colleague with PTSD. Someone who needed a chance to heal without pressure.

And that was exactly what she hadn't done.

Reality was crushing her. She'd just acted like some weird kind of teenager. He'd in-advertently highlighted something that she felt was a shortcoming of her own, and she'd lashed out. It may not have been deliberate but it had been her natural reaction. The old *not good enough* feelings washed over her.

She hated everything she was learning about herself tonight. She had to get her act together. She had to get over herself.

Because when Travis had walked out the door, he'd taken a big chunk of her heart with him.

The report was finished. He read it over for the twentieth time. It wasn't just good, it was excellent. Better than he could ever have hoped for.

His stomach was still doing flip-flops, his finger hovering over the button to press Send. He'd seen the expression on her face last night when he'd told her Aileen had warned there was a chance the nightmares might never go away. He'd wanted to find a different kind of way to give her that news. But she'd put him on the spot and he only wanted to be honest with her.

He scanned the accompanying email and pressed Send. He did still wonder if questions might be asked, but he was confident he'd given Ivy the best recommendation he could.

His sisters had been all over him last night, instantly catching the vibe that things weren't going well. He couldn't talk to them. None of them knew about his PTSD and he could only imagine the reaction if he told them. His family were like a wrap-around blanket. He wouldn't be able to move for them, and right now what he needed was space.

Actually, not true. What he needed was Ivy. But it felt as though she was slipping away from him like grains of sands sliding through his fingers. And it was all his fault. He should have dealt with this as soon as he'd first recognised the signs. He shouldn't have let it fester and take hold for four years. And now? When he'd met a woman he actually wanted to build a future with, it might just be too late.

Aileen had talked about more than he'd revealed to Ivy. She'd asked him about his navy career—then about triggers. He hadn't thought about it before. But apparently Aileen had noticed that in certain situations she seemed to lose Travis for a second.

He'd been horrified. Because he hadn't recognised it for himself. On her advice, he'd started keeping a diary. Thinking back and recording which nights his nightmares seemed worse, along with key events in the previous days. She'd found a pattern. A pattern they'd discussed at length.

He didn't like what he was discovering. He didn't like the fact the job he'd always loved might actually be enabling his condition.

But, deep down, he knew that was what his mind had been telling him all along. It was why he'd started to respond to Peters's emails.

It was as if he'd known the only way to heal was to get out.

Travis had gone into the ward that day to a full clinic of patients. Ivy was on duty but they'd both been so busy their paths hadn't crossed.

The boom came out of nowhere, reverberating through the metal carrier.

He didn't even think. His body acted instinctively, crouching on the floor as if he were hiding behind that stone wall again as the enemy let loose with a hail of bullets.

For a few seconds he relived past events. The fear, the terror, the adrenaline, the sweat, the roaring in his ears as if all other noise had disappeared.

Ivy appeared in front of him, her face close to his, her hand on his cheek. 'Travis, Travis, come back to me. You're okay.'

He could see her blonde hair and green eyes. But even though her lips were clearly moving, his brain couldn't make sense of the words. It was as if the whole world was slipping all around him.

She lifted her other hand to cup his other cheek. Her words seemed to be coming out of a fog. 'Travis. Look at me. *Look at me.* There's an accident on the flight deck. I have to go.

But I need to make sure you're okay. Tell me you're okay.'

A pack was dumped right next to him, landing on the floor with a loud thump.

It brought him back to reality. Tony was already running for the door. 'Come on, Trav!' he yelled over his shoulder.

Things came back into focus. 'What…?' he asked Ivy.

She was shaking. The hands that were on his cheeks were trembling. 'Flight deck,' she said slowly. 'There's an accident. All hands.' The emergency siren was wailing.

Something clicked into place in his brain. He stood up, grabbing the pack and starting to run after Tony.

As he pounded along the grey corridors up towards the flight deck he could hear her running behind him. He couldn't believe what had just happened to him. That had *never* happened before.

He wanted to stop. He wanted to throw himself inside his cabin, slam the door behind him and try to work out why he'd had such a strong flashback. It might have only been a few seconds, but he'd been there. Back behind the wall, listening to the bullets ricocheting. Feeling the warm belly of his friend as he'd tried to stem the bleeding. His head turning from side to side as he tried to determine who he could help, and who there would be no chance for. It was probably the most sickening memory that he had. And he'd been right back there. Living it again.

Instead, he was running down the corridor, catching up with Tony as they took the stairs three at a time. A boom like that could only mean one thing. A crash on the flight deck.

Tony threw open the door and the wind that hit them was incredible. The sight was worse. The smell of burning oil. Warm orange flames licking the air. Crew on the deck. Foam and hoses already out. Twisted metal.

Travis prioritised. There were parts of the jet scattered across the flight deck. The cockpit was mainly intact and the pilot was still in his seat. Men were crowded around, trying to prise it open.

His team was by his side, Tony and Ivy racing forward with him. By the time they got there, the cockpit was covered in foam to stop it catching alight. Warm flames were flickering nearby from one of the wings, catching the high wind and coming dangerously close. Instructions were also being lost in the wind.

One of the crew lost his footing and started tumbling towards the edge of the deck. Tony dived, his whole body weight landing on his fellow crew member to stop him being blown overboard in a powerful gust of wind.

Travis felt a hand grab the belt at his waist. He looked over his shoulder. Ivy. She could barely keep upright and was using him as an anchor.

'Move!' Travis yelled to the crew member right ahead of him. The young man was trying to lever the cockpit open, but because he was slicked with foam and could barely keep his feet in the wind, he was failing miserably.

Travis put his hands on the large crowbar, gripping it tightly. It was wedged where it should be. Every muscle in his body strained as he put all his weight and strength behind it. Another man closed in between him and Ivy, pushing Ivy sideways to allow himself to press up against Travis's back and mirror his position. His hands closed over the top of Travis's and crushed down with his added weight.

This time a tiny gap appeared in the seal around the cockpit. The smell of leaking jet fuel was becoming more pronounced by the second. 'Again!' yelled Travis. He had no idea who was behind him, but the guy was the muscle that he needed. They applied leverage again, and again. Another few crew members appeared alongside him, Ivy lost in the crush. He felt her hand release at his belt.

The other crew wedged their tools in next to his, and together they all repeated the motions. Finally, the cockpit cracked open, catching in the wind with such momentum that it struck a small blonde person on the other side. The crack could be heard above the wind.

It took him a millisecond to realise who the small blonde was. Travis was torn. A collar was pressed into his hands for the pilot and he started yelling, 'Ivy! Ivy! Someone check on Ivy!'

He put the collar on in less than a few seconds. The pilot was unconscious. And even though he really didn't want to be there, Travis did exactly what he should. Checked the pilot's pulse, airway, and ran his hands over the man's chest, back and limbs, checking for any obvious injuries before they moved him. It only took a few seconds before he was handed a knife to slice the harness then secured the pilot's head until they could slide him onto a stretcher. He kept his hands and the pilot's body perfectly aligned as he yelled to Tony, who he couldn't even see. 'Give me an update on her!'

It seemed to take ages to get the pilot securely onto the portable stretcher and for Tony's head to appear back in Travis's line of vision.

Travis's heart thundered in his chest. If he'd been more with it when the plane had crashed, he might have issued other orders that would have meant Ivy would have remained below decks. If he'd had time to concentrate—instead of focusing on releasing the pilot—he might have realised she'd slipped around the other side and into the path of the hood of the cockpit. If he'd delegated this task to Tony, he could be doing what he really wanted to do—checking on Ivy.

If…

Something struck him hard, like a blow to the chest.

Tony's head bobbed up. 'She's okay. Just a bad knock on the head. She'll need a few stitches.' His voice drifted away in the strong wind.

Travis knew what he had to do next. Even though it hurt his heart.

He looked up at his fellow crew members, gripping the sides of stretcher. 'Sick bay!' he yelled, and they all took off, running to the door.

CHAPTER THIRTEEN

HER HEAD WAS pounding and she knew she was heading for another migraine. Tony had stitched her wound and sent her back to her quarters, but she was anxious to see Travis so she slipped into his office and waited.

He was still working on assessing the unconscious pilot. It was an anxious time for everyone on board. Ivy had already heard that even though the winds had been gale force, the pilot had been cleared to land. As he'd landed, his plane had caught the tail end of a squall—notorious in the Pacific—almost flipping his plane over and making one wing catch the flight deck and causing him to crash.

She could almost have heard a pin drop outside as everyone moved silently while doing their jobs, all praying the pilot would regain consciousness soon.

Ivy wished she could help but knew that right now she would probably be a hindrance.

She was worried about Travis and what she'd witnessed earlier. His PTSD was worse than she'd ever imagined. She'd seen those few seconds when he'd flashed back to somewhere else. It had been real to him. She had seen the flash of fear, the way his skin had prickled, his defensive posture and the rapid pulse at the base of his throat. For the briefest of seconds she'd wondered if she could actually bring him back at all.

She'd been scared for him. Scared that he was reliving one of his worst experiences all over again.

But she couldn't pretend that part of her mind hadn't wondered if he should be doing this job. She hated herself. She really did. But if she hadn't been there to recognise what had happened and bring him back, how long would Travis have been frozen? What if another doctor hadn't been around to take the lead on the rescue? It didn't even bear thinking about.

Ivy leaned back in Travis's chair, contemplated for a few seconds then put her feet on the desk. She did feel a bit woozy and wanted to close her eyes for a few minutes. Give herself a chance not to think about all the stuff she probably needed to. Her feet accidentally knocked his laptop and the screen flickered on. It was open at his emails, and Ivy pulled her feet back down and stuck her hands out to automatically press the functions to lock the machine.

But her hands froze.

There was an email on-screen with her name on it. Her recommendation for SMO.

Her heart twisted in her chest. She knew she shouldn't look. Of course she shouldn't look. But who wouldn't when it was right in front of them?

She pressed her lips together and scanned the text. She was only past the first few sentences when every muscle in her body tensed and she stood up. Travis hadn't written her recommendation.

He hadn't written it.

Her head started to swim. She stopped reading.

It was standard procedure to ask the senior officer for a report on a candidate for promotion. It was unheard of for the senior officer to delegate that task to someone else.

If Travis hadn't written her recommendation it would raise red flags. And people could jump to conclusions about her fitness to practise, her personal conduct, her suitability for the job.

It didn't matter which one out of these was actually true. The fact he'd not written her recommendation would send a big enough message for people to ask questions. And in the navy mud and rumour had a nasty habit of sticking.

Travis King had just ruined her career.

There was only one reason for that. He didn't think she was good enough to be an SMO.

For a moment she couldn't breathe. Why would he do that to her? Why?

Didn't he want her to be promoted? Was he trying to keep her next to him or, worse than that, junior to him?

How dared he?

Her head was already thudding, waves of nausea enveloping her as tears pricked her eyes. She'd thought she loved this man. She'd contemplated a future with him. She'd even had a few wild thoughts about him proposing and them finding a place together back in San Diego. She must have been crazy.

The pain in her chest was so real. She'd had dreams, for herself and for them. And it felt as if they'd been whipped out from underneath her without a second's notice. Anger surged through her veins, along with a wave of devastation and hurt. He'd all but told her he loved her. Why would he do this?

Why wouldn't he sit her down and have an

actual conversation with her, if he thought she wasn't suitable for promotion?

The hateful words swirled around in her brain again. *Not good enough. Not good enough.*

The door creaked and Ivy looked up. Travis appeared at the door, his face creased in a smile but with worry in his eyes. 'I was looking for you. I wanted to check on you. I'm so sorry. The last thing I wanted was for you to get hurt.'

He moved over swiftly next to her, lifting his hands to her brow.

She flinched and moved back. 'Don't touch me,' Ivy hissed.

He pulled his hands back and his brow wrinkled. 'Ivy? I'm sorry, it was the wind. Well, and me. I was focusing on getting our pilot out. I didn't realise you'd gone around the other side, or that the wind would catch the hood.'

'I'm not talking about this,' she said coldly, pointing to her brow. 'I'm talking about this.' She pointed her finger at the screen of his computer. She didn't care at all that his emails were private. She wasn't at all embarrassed about snooping—because she hadn't been.

'What are you talking about?' Travis looked genuinely confused.

She spun the laptop around. 'This, the recommendation you gave me—or didn't give me, as it happens. Why would you do this? You know how badly I wanted promotion. And right up until you did this I thought I was in the running.' She pressed her hand to her heart. 'And I thought you would want to support me. But no. You've deliberately thrown a spanner in the works. The man who said he cared for me, the man I loved too, has just ruined my career!'

Angry tears spilled down her cheeks. 'I'll never forgive you for this. If you didn't think I was up to the task, you should have had the decency, and balls, to sit me down and tell me.'

She bent her head and gripped the desk as a mixture of dizziness and nausea swept over her. She should be lying down. She knew that. But what she'd discovered was too important. It couldn't wait.

His hand brushed against her arm. 'Ivy, no—'

But she cut him dead. 'I helped you, I supported you when we both know that you shouldn't be functioning as an SMO right now. Not with the effects of your PTSD.' She stepped forward to him, rage enveloping her. 'I didn't tell anyone you weren't fit for duty. I made a mistake. I won't make that mistake again.'

Travis's eyes widened in horror at her harsh words.

She couldn't quite believe they'd come out of her mouth. But Ivy was no pushover.

Only a few hours ago she'd cradled his cheek in the palm of her hand, knowing he was lost to his monsters. She'd been duty-bound to report that and yet it hadn't even occurred to her. Because that was not the type of person she was.

This was the guy she loved. She wanted him to get better. She'd wanted him to get help for himself, and for them, and she'd planned to wait by his side while it happened. Her heart squeezed inside her chest. With love came trust.

Everything was gone.

Travis was stunned. He'd gone to locate Ivy but couldn't find her. His office had been the last resort and he'd been so relieved to see her at his desk.

Now her words left his head spinning. But what was worse was the look in her eyes.

He shook his head fiercely. 'No, Ivy. No. I thought long and hard about that recommendation. I even spoke to Tony about it. I want you to get that job—of course I do. You deserve it. But this?' He held up his hands. 'Us? Our timing sucked, and the last thing I wanted to do was give you a glowing recommendation that someone could cast a shadow on and say it was biased because we're in a relationship. I was stuck between a rock and a hard place because I know what it looks like when an SMO doesn't give a colleague a recommendation.

'So… I had to think of an alternative. You're a team player, Ivy. It was one of the first things I noticed about you. And I like it, it's a skill that not all surgeons have. Did you look at your recommendation? Did you read it? Mine is there, alongside a dozen others. It's the best recommendation you could ever get. Everyone thinks you should get the job. And if we are asked questions at a later date about when our relationship started, we can be honest. Things have overlapped. We can declare things. Or at least I thought we could.'

He shook his head, a confused expression on his face. 'Why would you think I think you're not good enough? That's just crazy. You're more than qualified for this job.'

The words she'd hissed at him were still being processed in his brain. She'd threatened to report him and his condition. She'd told him he wasn't fit to do the job. He was automatically and instantly offended and couldn't pretend not to be.

'You want to report me?' he asked her. 'Do

it!' The response came out harsher than he intended it to. 'Report me. I froze. Yes. I froze. I admit it. But I still managed to get out there. I still managed to do my job—just like I have every day for the last four years. Should I be SMO when I have PTSD? Who knows? That's for the navy to decide. But if you don't think I'm fit for duty, say so. Don't put the safety of anyone on this ship at risk for my sake.'

He couldn't think straight. She was right in front of him, clearly not feeling well. He could see how she was holding on to the desk. She had a dressing on her head covering her stitches. Her blonde hair was dishevelled, her face flushed. Those green eyes that had flirted and teased him for the last few weeks seemed to have some kind of shield in front of them. There had been a definite flash of anger but now she looked numb. As if she couldn't believe where they'd both got to.

He couldn't either.

Last night he'd listened to his heart. He'd emailed Peters and told him he was definitely considering a change from the navy. The conversation with Aileen had struck chords exactly the way it should have. He had to accept his condition, his diagnosis, and do everything he could to heal. He would do it for himself and for the woman that he had fallen in love with.

He knew all about Ivy's career ambitions and supported them. But he was wise enough to know that both of them working for the navy would create challenges for a relationship—particularly if their spells of deployment were one after the other. His priority was to make their relationship work. He was beginning to see the light of being permanently based in San Diego. Or he'd thought he had. Now all those thoughts seemed to have vanished in a puff of smoke—or a bang on the head, as it were.

They stared at each other. Resentment simmered just under the surface. This woman, the woman he'd dreamed of spending a future with, the woman he'd risked his heart on, and who he had asked to wait for him. She was looking at him with hurt in her eyes. He'd done that to her.

He should apologise. Beg her to understand his reasoning. But as the colour drained from her face he realised he couldn't stand there and bicker back and forth with her. Ivy clearly needed to rest.

She gave a little twitch and looked at him. This time her voice was quiet. 'You're not the person I thought you were, Travis.' His gaze watched a single tear track down her face and he clenched his hands into fists to stop himself from reaching out and brushing it away.

'I'm me,' he replied instinctively. 'I've never claimed to be perfect. I can only be me. The person with baggage, and the guy who loves you. I have *never* done anything to deliberately hurt you or stand in your way.'

She remained silent, still gripping the desk with her hands before she took a deep breath and looked him in the eye.

It was like someone sticking their hand through his solar plexus and ripping his heart clean out of his chest.

'I wish I could believe that,' she said, before turning and walking out the door on shaky legs.

CHAPTER FOURTEEN

AILEEN GAVE HER a sideways glance. 'Ivy, do you want to talk?'

Ivy was busy writing a prescription for a patient she'd just seen and hadn't even heard Aileen come up alongside her.

'No,' was her automatic response, then she breathed and looked at Aileen again. 'Why would you ask me that?'

Aileen smiled and gestured to the tablet Ivy had in her hands. 'Because you've been standing here for the last five minutes, and you've started that prescription three times, and...' she leaned over Ivy's shoulder '...you still haven't completed it.'

Ivy sighed and put the tablet down on the counter.

'I don't think we can talk,' she said, her throat feeling dry.

'Try me,' said Aileen.

Ivy had barely spoken to anyone in the last

few days. She'd been ignoring calls from Liz and her family. She'd been giving monosyllabic answers and instructions to her co-workers. If Travis was in a room, she walked out. It was painful. Everything about him reminded her about the dreams she'd had.

She closed her eyes for a second and whispered, 'Is it enough if I tell you I can't wait to get off this ship?'

She didn't want to put things into words. Because then, depending on her mood, she either felt like a fool and a pushover, a heartless monster or a career-driven bitch. And every one of those thoughts amplified those not-good-enough feelings. She had judged herself to be all of those things over the last few days. She could barely eat, she couldn't sleep, and if she set foot outside her cabin, she ran the risk of running into Travis.

Her job chances were shot. But if she put in for a transfer right now, or requested to be reassigned, it would throw more red flags on her record. On top of her 'not' recommendation, that was the last thing she needed.

'You know anything you tell me is confidential,' Aileen said quietly.

Ivy turned her head quickly. 'But I'm not your patient,' she said, with an element of panic.

Aileen gave a soft laugh and held out one hand. 'Ivy, everyone on board is my patient, just like they are yours.' She gave a thoughtful pause. 'Why don't you just let me be your friend?'

Ivy felt tears brim in her eyes for the thousandth time. A friend was exactly what she needed right now. But she didn't want to involve anyone else on the ship in this. People had already noticed the atmosphere between her and Travis. She had witnessed the exchange of glances between staff and the way they were tiptoeing around her.

'I can't, Aileen,' she breathed. 'If I talk about it to you, then it's real. And I don't want it to be.'

Aileen leaned close and squeezed Ivy's hand. 'Door is always open,' she whispered, before she moved away.

It took Ivy a few moments to collect herself. She had a patient to see. She had to pull herself together and get a grip.

An hour later Tony came into the treatment room as Ivy was dispensing some drugs for a patient. He folded his arms and looked at her.

'What happened?'

'What do you mean?'

'Travis is leaving.'

The tablets she was trying to count out tumbled to the floor. 'What…?'

Tony was still looking at her.

'What do you mean, he's leaving?'

The phone next to her started ringing so she picked it up. 'Ivy Ross.'

'Flight Surgeon Ross, the captain needs to see you. Report to his office immediately.'

Panic swept through her. She hadn't been ordered to speak to the captain at all on this trip. If he was calling her to his office, something was wrong.

Tony must have noticed the expression on her face. 'What's wrong?'

'I'm to report to the captain.' Her voice was trembling.

Tony gave a shrug. 'Makes sense.'

She was confused. 'Why?'

Tony glanced at his watch. 'Because Travis leaves any second now. You're about to be promoted to SMO. You were in the running for the next job. Makes sense to give it to you now.'

There was a roaring in her ears. Every cell in her body was on fire. Everything about this was so wrong. It looked as if it seemed entirely normal to Tony. But none of this seemed normal to Ivy.

'What do you mean, he's leaving now? Right now?'

Tony nodded. 'He's probably already taken off.'

She was running. She didn't even stop to explain. Her feet were pounding down the slim corridors. 'Move!' she yelled at a few seamen to clear the way.

She climbed up ladders, heading to the flight deck as quickly as she could.

She needed to see him. She had to talk to him. Every hour of every day she felt something different about what had happened between them. It didn't make sense to her. But the one thing that hadn't changed was how she felt in her heart. She loved this guy. She loved Travis King. And she didn't want to leave things like this.

She wasn't allowed on the flight deck if take-offs or landings were taking place. But she flung open the door anyway.

As the wind whipped around her, her stomach plummeted. A helicopter was already rising high into the sky. Even from here she could recognise the familiar shape in the passenger seat. His helmet showed he was looking in another direction. She waved her hands frantically, trying to signal him.

But Travis was deep in conversation with the pilot next to him.

He didn't even see her. Didn't even know that she'd come to talk to try and catch him before he left.

Ivy was left in the middle of the empty flight deck, caught in a flurry of wind, as the man she loved disappeared out of sight.

CHAPTER FIFTEEN

Ten weeks later

'Travis, there's a last-minute patient. She's insisting she needs to be seen today. She asked for you by name. Can you fit her in?'

Travis finished typing preoperative notes on the last patient that he'd seen. It was only 5:00 p.m., and while he knew his secretary wanted to finish for the day, he wasn't anxious to get home. 'Sure, no problem. And, Mel? You can go on home. I'll close up.'

'You sure?' He could hear the happiness in her voice through the intercom and could only imagine how much she was smiling right now.

'Of course.'

Travis finished his notes and stood up, walking over to the large window overlooking part of San Diego Bay. Peters had delivered on everything he'd promised. The partnership, the office and work that he wanted to do. He'd already seen a number of army and navy veterans with ongoing health issues.

The normal resignation process of six months had been negotiated due to his existing PTSD. He would remain in the navy reserves, but had been granted permission to take up another role while his paperwork was processed.

From here he could still see part of the fleet moored in San Diego Bay. It was like watching family and friends from afar. He loved this city. He would always stay here, and he was slowly getting used to what his new life would be.

He realised he hadn't even asked Mel anything about the new patient as he walked to the door of the waiting room.

The woman had her back to him. She'd clearly been pacing and was currently staring out at the view in the same way that he had been.

Travis's skin prickled. He didn't need to ask her name. He knew it.

Ivy.

She froze. She had clearly heard him coming into the room. She turned slowly to face him.

Her hair was sleek and smooth, and she was wearing her navy uniform.

'Hi.' Her voice was nervous and slightly croaky.

'Hi.' Ten weeks. It had been ten weeks since he'd last seen her, when she'd accused him of wrecking her job chances and not being fit for duty.

The last action he'd taken before leaving the *Coolidge* had been to recommend her for the job he was vacating.

He was sure that right now his heart was swelling in his chest as memories flooded through him. The way she'd looked at him like a patient the night she'd realised he had PTSD. She'd phoned this office as a potential patient. That was how he had to treat her. No matter what his heart dictated.

He dropped into professional mode and gestured to the office behind him. 'Come through. What can I do for you?'

He'd turned and started walking already. Trying to collect his thoughts for a moment as he held the door for her.

Ivy pressed her lips together. She strode past him in a wave of orange blossom. The scent sent a shock wave through his system. Memories of her lips, her skin pressing against his.

He did his best not to let his attention be captured by her silhouette.

He waited until she sat down and then moved around the desk to sit opposite. He was nervous. She'd sent him a few texts after he'd left, but he hadn't replied.

Travis licked his lips. 'You requested me by name. Can I assume you're here as a patient?'

Ivy took her time to reply. She shook her head. 'I landed just over an hour ago. My bags are down the hall. This is my first stop.'

He straightened in his chair. Her assignment on the *Coolidge* must have just finished. She kept going. 'I have my next deployment details.'

She pushed a letter across the table to him. He glanced down. SMO on another aircraft carrier. It would last twelve weeks.

'Congratulations.' His voice was cold. He knew that. 'You got your promotion.'

She leaned forward a little. 'I got my promotion because they told me mine was the most inclusive recommendation they'd ever seen. They are thinking of using a more three-sixty approach to recommendations in the future. They realised it's important that everyone can give feedback on a candidate, not just their superior officer.'

Travis was still. He'd heard she'd got her promotion but hadn't asked any details. He'd still been unsure if what he'd done had been the right move for Ivy or not.

He gave the briefest nod of his head but didn't speak.

'I came to say I'm sorry. I'm sorry I lost my temper with you and misjudged you. I didn't expect you to leave. I thought... I thought that at some point on the ship we'd get a chance to talk again. Re-evaluate things.'

'But I was doing a job you didn't think I was fit to do.'

She froze, her eyes darting away from his. When she looked back she pressed her hand on her heart. 'I'm sorry, I should never have said that. You're a wonderful doctor, Travis.'

He shook his head. 'You were right. I needed to make a choice to get better. Aileen had already spoken to me about how continuing in the navy was probably triggering things for me. I hadn't taken the time to think things through. Even though, subjectively, I think I'd already figured that out. Now...' he glanced out the window again '... I have taken time to think things through properly. That's why I'm here.'

'And that's why I'm here.'

He furrowed his brow. 'What?'

'I'm here because I've had ten weeks to drive myself crazy in the middle of the Pacific Ocean. About how I can say sorry to the man I love. The man I should have told there would be no need for waiting, that I would stay by his side while he got treatment. The man I should have told that, whether his treatment worked or not, I would always be by his side.'

He stiffened and shook his head but Ivy continued.

'I want you to get better, Travis, of course I do. But I should never have walked away. I should have stayed by your side, right from the start.'

'There's a chance that I'll never be better,' he said softly. Those words were hard to say out loud. But ten weeks away from Ivy and ten weeks of counselling had made him realise it was important to be honest. 'You should feel safe to be with the person you love.'

In the blink of an eye Ivy moved around the desk to be by his side. 'Travis, I do feel safe around you. I've had a long time to think about this. My heart keeps telling me the same thing. I have to be with the person I love. You are a good man. If you spend your nights having nightmares, we'll find a way to deal with it. I can sleep in another bed, although I'd much rather be in your arms. And if you have a nightmare, I'll be there to support you when you wake up.'

She sighed and reached out to take his hands.

'A number of years ago someone I loved told me I wasn't good enough. It doesn't matter that you never, ever made me feel like that. I had my own issues that I hadn't admitted. I always had the little voice in the back of my head, and when I thought you hadn't backed me for the job, all those feelings came flooding back. I've had weeks to think about that, and Aileen has been a great friend and support. She made me realise I had to work through those things and face up to reality.

'And the reality is, I love you, Travis King. You're a good man. The best man I've ever met and the one I want to have in my future—however that looks.'

Travis sucked in a long, slow breath. 'Ivy, I can't pretend I was happy when you told me I couldn't do my job. But you were right, and I knew I had to step away. I've been seeing a counsellor for the last ten weeks and things seem to be going well. Will my nightmares ever stop for good? I don't know. Have I thought about you every day since I left the *Coolidge*? Of course I have. But you thought I'd ruined your career, Ivy. The fact that you even considered I'd do something like that made me step back and wonder if you loved me like I love you.'

She went to speak but he shook his head.

'You see, Ivy, ever since I met you I've let my guard down. Because it seemed like the right thing to do. You were the first person I felt a real connection to. I lost my heart to you—right from the beginning—even when I knew I wasn't in a position to do that. When I thought that I'd hurt you I couldn't cope. I had to leave. I'd put off seeking treatment for my PTSD too long. I requested an emergency leave of absence and resigned from the navy. I was lucky they agreed to my request and let me leave early.'

He paused for a second. She was watching him intently, her hands still in his. 'The truth is I had wondered if I'd ever get the chance to meet someone and have something other than the navy in my life. I'd been approached a few times about going into private practice but had never even considered the possibilities. Here?' He pulled one hand from hers and held it upwards. 'I joined on the agreement that this company would offer services to veterans. I've done three surgeries every week so far. Mainly follow-ups on injuries received in service, a few surgeries on back and hip problems—long-term damage from the job.'

He looked out at the view across the bay. 'It feels good to be here. I'm getting used to sleeping in my own bed at night.' He licked his lips and looked at her again. 'But there's something missing.' His gaze locked with hers. 'A huge part of my heart.'

Ivy was glad she'd changed position. She was kneeling next to Travis's chair right now. If she'd been standing, her legs would have been shaking. From the second she'd disembarked from the *Coolidge* and started on her long journey back home, she'd had one thing on her mind. Seeing Travis King again.

She was sure he'd hate her. He hadn't answered a single one of her messages—and she didn't blame him. But she had to be here. She had to be by his side. The longer they'd been apart, the more sure she'd become. Her earlier flurry of anger had disappeared. Her rational brain had kicked in, and she'd never felt so much like a villain in her life. She loved this guy. This was the guy she'd spent the last few years dreaming of meeting. Someone with whom the spark was so vibrant it could light up the sky. Someone who had captured her mind, and her heart.

Aileen had talked her through her feelings of inadequacy, the thoughts of never being good enough, and she'd realised she had to let them go if she ever wanted to live the life she should.

She kept holding Travis's hand. Now she

was here she didn't want to let go. 'Travis, I'm so sorry. All the dreams that you mention, and feeling like you're missing a piece of your heart? I feel exactly the same. Since you left, nothing has felt good. Nothing has felt right. I know what I would be asking of you. I know that this time it would be me asking you to wait—to wait while I go on assignments that will last months. We never discussed things like this. And I don't even know if that's the kind of future you imagined for us.' She blinked and swallowed the huge lump in her throat. 'But if it's not, I understand.'

He gave her an odd look. 'If you hadn't got the job, if you hadn't been given the promotion, what would you have done?'

She didn't hesitate for a second. 'This. I would still be right here.' Ivy took an enormous breath. 'I love my job—you know I do. I thought career was everything, and then I met you and realised my job didn't define me. I want a life I can live and enjoy. I want to be with the person that I love. And I have to work to make that happen. You've managed to create a new life outside the navy, and I can do that too.'

His voice was low. 'I wouldn't ask you to.'

She pressed her lips together. 'That's because you put me first. And I need to do the same. I need to put you first. If you're willing to give me a second chance, we can work at it. I can try this first assignment. If things don't work out, I'll look at other career pathways. Ones that mean I can be by your side every single night.'

He gave a soft shake of his head. 'I'm not your patient.'

She smiled at him, noticing the tiny lines at the sides of his blue eyes. 'No, but you are my one true love. And hopefully one day you'll be the father of my children.'

His eyes crinkled in amusement. 'Are we going from blind date to children in one fell swoop?'

She shrugged. 'We've wasted enough time. A really wise woman told me that when you know, you know.'

His eyebrows rose. 'Who said that?'

'Your sister.'

His eyebrows went even higher. 'You've been talking to my sister?' Then he gave her a sideways glance, as if scared to ask the next question. 'Which one?'

'All three. They're quite a lethal combination. When you wouldn't answer my messages I contacted them all. I told them it was all my fault. And that I wanted to make things up to you.'

He gave a quiet laugh. 'Now I understand why they haven't been constantly pestering me about you.'

She gave a nod and finally let go of his hands, holding hers out. 'Think of this a recreation of our blind date. You'd just come back from deployment and the first thing you did when you arrived back in San Diego was to message me to meet. I've been waiting ten weeks to do this. It's been the longest ten weeks of my life.' She laughed and tilted her head to one side. 'Remember all the eighties and nineties movies we talked about?'

He nodded and she grinned. 'Then all I'll say is I'm just a girl, standing in front of a guy I love, asking him to love me.'

Her heart was fluttering in her chest, wondering what Travis would say.

He stood up, gave her a smile and pulled her close. 'I think he might say, I love you right back, Ivy Ross. Best blind date *ever*!'

EPILOGUE

THERE WAS ONLY one place they could possibly get married. The hotel on Coronado Island was famous and the gardens were currently packed with half of San Diego's resident navy personnel, alongside Travis and Ivy's families and friends.

'Ready?' asked Travis as he slid up the zip on her satin wedding dress.

They'd decided not to be traditionalists. Ivy's next deployment was in a few weeks and they wanted to spend as much time together as possible. She picked up her bouquet of orange blossoms and dark green leaves and turned to face her soon-to-be husband in his tuxedo.

She straightened his tie. 'Well, hello, handsome.' She smiled. Outside the grounds were crowded with many of their friends in uniform, but Travis didn't seem the least bit bothered that he was wearing something different.

He interlinked his fingers with hers as the

sound of clinking glasses from the gardens drifted up towards them.

'Let's get out there and join in the fun.' He smiled.

'Can't wait,' she replied.

There was a huge cheer as they walked down the staircase and out into the gardens and shaded arboretum with an arch of flowers.

Travis's parents and his three sisters were at the front of the crowd, dressed in bright colours, with Ivy's parents and brother and sister at the other side of the aisle. His brother was his best man, and Ivy's brother's kids were already off playing in a corner of the garden, smearing dirt on their yellow outfits.

Isaiah Bridges gave her a nod as they walked down the aisle, from where he was sitting along with Tony, Aileen and a whole array of personnel from the *Coolidge*.

Ivy's father stood to give her away and the gardens fell silent as they recited their vows. Love, honour and obey in sickness and health had special meaning for them. Travis was still on his journey but making good progress.

As the celebrant finished the service, Travis bent to kiss her. 'When are we talking about babies again?' he whispered.

'That ship might have sailed.' She winked as a nearby waiter appeared with a silver tray of champagne and she lifted a glass at one side. 'Secret lemonade. Let everyone else think it's champagne.'

His eyes widened. 'Really?'

She nodded and grinned. 'Really.'

Travis clasped his arms around her waist and spun her then lifted his own glass from the tray and raised it in the sky. 'Everyone, I'd like to raise a glass to Ivy King, my blind-date bride!'

* * * * *

If you enjoyed this story, check out
these other great reads from
Scarlet Wilson

Family for the Children's Doc
Cinderella and the Surgeon
Just Friends to Just Married?
Healing the Single Dad's Heart

All available now!